KU-215-840

# My Story

# BLOODY TOWER

## Valerie Wilding

**SCHOLASTIC**

For my mother – always a tower of strength

While the events described and some of the characters in this book
may be based on actual historical events and real people, Tilly
Middleton is a fictional character, created by the author, and her
diary is a work of fiction.

Scholastic Children's Books
Euston House, 24 Eversholt Street,
London, NW1 1DB, UK
A division of Scholastic Ltd
London ~ New York ~ Toronto ~ Sydney ~ Auckland
Mexico City ~ New Delhi ~ Hong Kong

First published in the UK by Scholastic Ltd, 2002
This edition published by Scholastic Ltd, 2008

Text copyright © Valerie Wilding, 2002
Cover illustration © Richard Jones, 2008

ISBN 978 1407 10477 5

All rights reserved

Typeset by M Rules
Printed in the UK by CPI Bookmarque, Croydon, CR0 4TD

4 6 8 10 9 7 5

The right of Valerie Wilding to be identified as the author of
this work has been asserted by her in accordance with the
Copyright, Designs and Patents Act, 1988.

This book is sold subject to the condition that it shall not, by way of trade
or otherwise be lent, resold, hired out, or otherwise circulated without the
publisher's prior consent in any form of binding or cover other than that
in which it is published and without a similar condition, including this
condition, being imposed upon the subsequent purchaser.

London, England
1553

# 2nd May 1553

This is my book. It was not always mine. Long ago, someone very important gave it to Father, and told him to give it to a lady. My mother can read a little, but cannot write, so he kept it for me. The paper is quite smooth and the colour of buttermilk, and my words are fairly neat and do not, I think, spoil it.

Father says I am unique, and should write about myself. I thought about my life and why I am unique. I live in the greatest castle in England – the Tower of London. It is a palace and a fortress, but it is also a prison. Our house is within the Tower walls so I soon hear about everything that goes on! I am the only girl of my age here. Indeed, there is only one other person near my age, and that is Tom, funny Tom, from the Royal Menagerie by the Tower gates, where the King's beasts are kept. Tom is almost fourteen and my best friend, but he stinks.

# 3rd May 1553

I had no time to write more yesterday. I was needed all day to help with the two little ones. Harry is teething and is cross and fretful. He bites everything he can reach, even me. Luckily, little Jack just smiles a lot, which is good for all of us! Mother is with child again and tires quickly. I told her I had begun to write my diary.

"You would do well to forget such nonsense, and spend more time learning important things," she said. "You cook like a farmer mixing compost."

Not true, but I did not say so, for fear of a sore head. Mother is quick with her hands when she is testy. Many times Father has had to prepare a salve for my bruises. It's fortunate that he is the Tower physician. Fortunate for me, though not for him. Sometimes he returns from attending a prisoner, and will not speak for an hour, but locks himself away in his study to work alone on his medicines. I think he sees bad things in the cells and down in the dungeons. My older brother, William, is newly apprenticed to Father, and has promised to tell me what goes on. He will not, I know. He never does.

# 5th May 1553

I tried to slip out to see Tom before dinner, but Mother chose today to clean the floors and remake the beds. She is too large to do it herself so I had to help Sal, our maidservant. William was sent for fresh rushes, while Sal and I swept out the smelly ones. William's share of the work was done then, so he went to help Father. While Sal spread new rushes over the floor, I took Harry and Jack to pick flower heads and herbs from our little garden to put with the rushes. They loved crawling around the floor mixing them all together. I got down on my hands and knees too, to put feverfew, tansy and some wormwood under the mattresses. I saved most for my own bed. My tiny room beneath the roof is quiet and all my own, but there are more lice and fleas up there than anywhere in the house, it seems, so I stuffed plenty of herbs beneath my mattress to keep them away. Anyway, I would rather sleep on my own with the lice than in the big bed with my small brothers. Sal sleeps on the truckle bed beside them and has to put up with Harry's night-time yells.

Mother cannot believe I wish to sleep here. "That room is

little more than a garret," she says, "and fit only for a servant." Ha! There is something I am keeping to myself. Although Mother can climb the ladder up to my room, she is too big to get right in through the hole in the floor!

## 7th May 1553

I told Tom about my book. He asked what it is called, and I said, "The Diary of Tilly Middleton." He wanted to know if I would put him in it. "It is only for interesting things," I said, but I was sorry afterwards that I had teased him, because he refused to show me the new lioness, which had come by ship from Africa. So? Who cares?

King Edward is ill, Father says. It seems to me he always is. It must be hard to be king when you are so young. What pleasure can he have? Kings have to talk all day with dull council men. Edward is not yet sixteen, and has ruled since he was nine. He's extremely serious, they say, and well educated, speaking Latin and French, and some Greek, Italian and Spanish, too. That is a lot of learning. His father, King Henry VIII, was a frightening man, it seems to me. Six wives! Two divorced, two beheaded, one died and the last, Queen Katherine Parr, outlived him. Father admired Katherine Parr.

He met her twice, and found her a clever, educated woman. He wanted his daughter to be like her, and that is why I have been well taught. I do not know that I am as clever, but I am not stupid, though William says otherwise.

## 8th May 1553

Tom showed me the lioness today. I knew he would. She is large and angry, and does not have a mane like the male lion. She has been kept in her travelling cage for too long, and is stiff in the legs. Tom is afraid of her. I am, too. The menagerie is only separated from the main Tower entrance by a bridge over the moat, so the Tower guards are all that is between those wild animals and me. Master Worsley, Keeper of the Royal Menagerie, visited today, so I could not stay long. If he saw me, he would tell Father and I would be in trouble for being there at all.

Tom says there will be many visitors tomorrow, wishing to see the lioness. He is pleased, because they will bring meat for the animals, and that saves him work. If they bring a small animal, dead or alive, they are admitted free.

I kept my skirt lifted off the floor so it would not trail in the dung. Mother sniffed when I came home, but said nothing other than, "Where have you been, you lazy creature? Take Jack and Harry out from under my feet."

So I took them to chase the ravens on Tower Green.

Father says the King is so ill he may not live. He has heard from the Royal physician that Edward could be dead by June. The poor boy has dreadful fits of the cough, and his spittle is sometimes green and sometimes black and sometimes pink – probably blood. I am sure my father could cure him. He cured a man whose foot was crushed by the new coin-press in the Royal Mint. Well, he did not cure his toes – they were mashed up like when a horse treads on a worm – but the man did live.

### 9th May 1553

Rain battered the roof all night and kept me awake. I spent much time thinking about poor King Edward. He has no child, and no younger brother, so if he dies, William says, the crown will go to his older sister, Mary. I asked Father if that is so, and he said it's true – it must go to one of the King's half-sisters – Princess Mary or Princess Elizabeth. . .

The Princess Elizabeth! I have not thought of her lately, yet I used to think of her often, and especially on September

7th, for we share a birthday. When I was little, I used to call her my princess! She is seven years older than me, and in her twentieth year. Sometimes I wish I was a princess myself. Elizabeth must have beautiful clothes and fine food and sleep in a silken bed, and walk in scented gardens. Then I remember that her mother's head was chopped off when she was only three. And now she is to lose her brother, Edward. I would not be a princess for all the riches in the world, if it meant losing my family – even William.

When my work in the house was done, I crossed the moat, left the Tower and strolled down to the river to watch the boats. Tom saw me go past the Lion Tower, where the menagerie is, and followed me. I smelt him before I saw him. When I told him we might soon have Queen Mary instead of King Edward, he made a face, "Master Worsley said that, too. He thinks there will be much trouble, because Princess Mary is a Catholic."

I will have to find out more.

## 10th May 1553

Two of Father's friends sat with him yesterday evening, drinking wine. Mother and I were by the window, listening.

As far as I can make out, there was a time when all of England was Catholic, and the Pope was head of the Church. Then King Henry VIII wished to divorce Princess Mary's mother, Catherine of Aragon, but the Pope said no. Henry sounds a fearsome man, because it seemed he would do anything to get his way. He decided that the Pope was no longer head of the Church in England, he, Henry, was! He declared that his marriage was unlawful and divorced Catherine. And since the marriage was not lawful, he said, Princess Mary was legally a bastard, which means she was born out of wedlock. Henry immediately married Anne Boleyn, who eventually gave birth to the Princess Elizabeth. Queen Anne behaved dreadfully badly, it is said, and she was beheaded – on Tower Green, right in the middle of my Tower of London. I could see the very spot from my room, except that I do not have a window, only a very little hole in the roof, directly above my mattress.

So Princess Mary is of the old religion, a Catholic, and Princess Elizabeth is of the new one – a Protestant.

But I'm confused. If Mary is a bastard, surely she cannot become queen? Oh, my head spins with it all. I shall forget it. Nothing princesses or queens do affects me. I say my prayers, and we all worship God in the way the men of the church order us to. Surely it does not matter whether our church is Catholic or Protestant. After all, God is God and no queen can change that.

The Royal family do not stay here at the Tower, as they

used to. Not since they cut off Anne Boleyn's head. King Edward came for a few weeks, just before his coronation, when I was about five, and I remember seeing him walking with his dogs on Tower Green. He looked very serious, and did not notice me.

I wonder if Mary will stay here before her coronation, too, once Edward is dead. I will ask Mother tomorrow, when we go to buy linen for the new baby.

## 11th May 1553

I have been in my garret for almost the whole day, with a huge pile of mending, a fat candle, one lump of bread and a cup of ale. Mother says I am a wicked girl to talk of the King's death, and William says I am stupid and deserve to be punished. I protested that Father had spoken of it, and discovered that my crime was to have spoken of it in the market place. Even Father would not dare talk loosely outside our home, they said.

How was I to know it is treason to talk of the King's death? How was I to know I could be put to death for doing so? Nobody told me. My candle is flickering and I can barely see to write. I am very hungry, and cannot stop crying.

# 14th May 1553

I have had nothing to write about for days, because I have not been allowed out of the house, except to feed the hens and weed the garden. Today is Sunday, so they had to let me out to go to church. I must not break that law, too. And if I have broken the law about speaking of the King's death, then I believe many men do. There was much whispering on Tower Green outside our chapel, St Peter's, today. I walked behind a group of Yeoman Warders and heard one talk about some of the prisoners being freed when "it" happens. I know exactly what "it" is. They mean that men imprisoned by Edward might be freed after the King dies, as long as they have not displeased Princess Mary.

I know that if I were anyone close to Mary at the moment, I would be busy being very pleasing to her!

# 16th May 1553

I have been so dreadfully bored today. All the time I was helping Sal make the bread, I was trying to work out how to get out of this place. It has been almost a week now. I am going mad and feel I want to burst. If I speak I am wrong, and if I do not speak I am told I am a sullen brat. I am glad of my diary. In this I can say what I want. Oh, what now?

## Later

It is the strangest thing and I am so intrigued. When I wrote those last words, I was angry at being disturbed simply to change Harry's linen (he dirties himself about a hundred times a day, it seems) and threw down my diary. Just now, I picked it up and found the spine bent, so that the book stayed open at some blank pages. As I tried to straighten it, I felt something beneath one of the pages. I looked and found, wedged tightly into where the pages join, a tiny folded paper, sealed with wax, and on it is some writing. There is an E followed by an L, but I cannot read the rest. The ink is smudged. I must think about this.


## 18th May 1553


At last, I am allowed out! I was sent into the city to collect a package for Father from the apothecary. It was wonderful to be among the crowds, and to see some life instead of being stuck in the house. The Tower, with all its goings-on, is quiet compared to the city, where everyone seems to shout all the time! The air was warm and still, and I could hear the roars of people at the bear-baiting pit on the other side of the river. I am glad I could not hear the roars of the bears, poor creatures.

A woman on a donkey shouted, "Here, lass," and threw me an apple from the basket she carried. I jumped and caught it, shouting my thanks to her, but when I looked, I saw it was rotten. She rode off, cackling with laughter, and I felt like throwing it at her. Instead I saved it to throw at someone in the pillory. Some thief or pickpocket is always locked up there for people to laugh and jeer at.

My arms were full of packages on the way home, so when a great crowd of boys came by, chasing some sort of ball, I jumped back out of the way into a convenient doorway. I wish I had not, because the door suddenly opened and a huge man sent me flying with one shove of his great belly. My foot slipped in a heap of fresh dog mess and down I tumbled. My hand went right in it. That was all right – I rinsed it in a puddle, but my skirt! I knew Mother would be angry, because we washed it only two weeks ago.

She was more than angry.

"Where have you been all this time?" she cried.

"Walking . . . the apothecary was slow. . ." I began, but she took one look at my stained skirt, screwed her nose up, and shouted, "You have been in the menagerie with that dung-boy!" I protested that I had not.

"I can smell him," she shouted, and boxed my ears. They still burn. Life is not fair.

Later I looked at the sealed paper again. I feel sure it is a letter. But from whom? And who is EL—? The only names I can think of that begin with E and L are Eliza, which is too short, and Elizabeth and Eleanor. But I do believe I can see the tail of a Z as it swoops downwards, though it is not all that clear.

## Later

A great and wonderful thought has come to me! Father said someone of importance gave the book to him. Could it have been the Princess Elizabeth? Is she the mysterious EL—? No. If the book had been hers, she would have known the letter was there and would have opened it. The seal is unbroken.

So perhaps the book belonged to someone who had written the letter to the Princess. I am sure it will be useless asking Father who the mysterious person of importance was. He never utters the name of any prisoner to us. He says that side of Tower life must stay outside our door. But I could try to find out more.

## 22nd May 1553

Sal said there was a lot of talk at the fish stall this morning about a wedding. "The Lady Jane Grey," she said, "did wed a son of the Duke of Northumberland yesterday. 'Tis said she did not want to, but her parents beat her until she agreed."

What a strange thing. My parents would not have to beat me to make me marry the son of a duke! Imagine, Lady Tilly – no! Lady Matilda. I would meet the king (or queen).

I asked Sal why this girl's wedding was so interesting, and she told me that Henry VIII was great-uncle to the Lady Jane, which makes her a sort of cousin of King Edward, so she could be in line for the throne. The King, we hear, is steadily pining away, and may die shortly. It is nearly June, after all.

Hah! Lady Jane might dream of the throne, but I should like to hear what the two princesses would say about that! Anyway, I do not know if any of this is true – Sal is always full of fanciful notions.

I wish that Tom would not talk to her – he is my friend.

## 31st May 1553

Mother slapped Sal today, and I for one am glad. My uncle, who is a Chief Yeoman Warder, had a puppy that died, so he took it early to the menagerie for the beasts and found Tom and Sal together, teasing the wolf. I hope it chews through the wooden slats of its cage and eats them. Mother said Sal had better think only of her work, or she will be turned out of the Tower.

I could not bear that to happen to me! Although sometimes it feels as if we are all in a prison, I would not wish to leave here, ever. It is my home, my safe home.

Father has been busy and irritable lately, and it was only today that I dared to ask him about my book. He said he attended a noble lady as she went to the block. The lady gave her possessions to her attendants, so that the executioner should not have them, then she pressed the book into Father's hands and said, "Take this . . . give it to a lady."

"I hope you care well for your book, Tilly," Father said. "It has passed through some of the most noble hands in the land."

## 1st June 1553

The whole day has been spent caring for the little ones, and helping Sal with the work of the house. Mother has pains in her belly. Father is anxious, but she does not want him near her. The midwife has called three times, and Mrs Nell from the Tower tavern is sitting with her. Maybe the baby will come too soon, like last time. I am frightened that Mother might die. I have just had a little cry and have prayed for Mother and the baby, and for myself, and feel better for it.

The boys are asleep and the house is quiet apart from Sal banging up and down the stairs below me. Now I have time to think about the "EL—" letter. Shivers run down my spine when I consider what it might contain. For I have reached a great conclusion. I am convinced that the noble lady whom Father attended was none other than Queen Anne Boleyn, the mother of the Princess Elizabeth. And if I had been Anne Boleyn, about to be beheaded, my thoughts would be of no one but the little child I was to leave behind.

I believe this tiny letter was to be smuggled out of the Tower. I think Father made a mistake. He was not to give it to any lady. He was supposed to give it to one of Anne Boleyn's own ladies (when they were safely outside the Tower walls) and she would see that it reached the Princess or was held for her until she was old enough to understand the contents.

I am tired, and keep falling into a daydream. I dream that I am the one to hand the letter to its rightful owner, the Princess Elizabeth.

# 23rd June 1553

I have been too busy and too tired and upset to write in my book. There are still just four children in our family – William, Harry, Jack and me. The baby, a girl, was born but did not live. She was called Susannah, and was baptized by the midwife. I do not know why it hurts me so much to think of her. I did not know her. I cannot even see her in my mind when I close my eyes. Everyone in the Tower has been so kind. That hurts me, too.

Today I went out for the first time in many days. Apart from the guards, I saw no one I knew as I passed through the Lion Tower, but on reaching Tower Hill I saw Tom coming towards me.

He did not stop. He did not smile or even look at me, but kept his eyes cast down. I suppose he just wants to be friends with Sal now, and not with me, although what he can find to interest him in a maidservant, I do not know. Mind, Mother says that to me about him. "What you can find interesting in the chatter of a boy who does nothing all day but shovel animal dung," she grumbles, "I cannot imagine."

I try to tell her he is just my friend – I am hardly going to marry him. She snorts when I say that. "Indeed you are not. Your father will decide who you marry, my girl."

"Then please let me be friends with Tom," I say. "I have no other friends near my age in the Tower."

Anyway, Tom does far more than shovel dung. He feeds the animals and makes sure the carpenter keeps the cages in good repair, so fine ladies and gentlemen can see the beasts in safety. Even the King may come, for the menagerie belongs to him. The King's safety is an important responsibility, so Tom is not just a dung-shoveller. Clearly, my mother does not understand this.

But the poor King will not come now because he is so ill, and I care not whether he comes here anyway. If Tom will not speak to me and be my friend, I will not visit the menagerie, either.

## 25th June 1553

Something strange is happening. At church, we prayed as usual for the health of the King, but when we came to the part where we normally pray for his half-sisters, Elizabeth and Mary, their names were not mentioned. After the service, men gathered in their groups as they always do, but today the groups were larger, and there were arguments and raised voices.

At dinner, William asked Father why Princess Mary's name was not mentioned. "After all, though I pray Almighty God will spare the King," he said, "we should surely pray for his successor."

Father looked serious. "All is not as it seems, William," he said. "The Lady Jane Grey is being talked of a great deal at Court."

"Talked of how?" asked William.

"She married the Duke of Northumberland's son, Guilford Dudley, not long ago."

"I heard that," I said, and wished I had not, when Father gave me a sharp look.

"Northumberland wishes to make his family great," he continued. "Indeed, he works hard to make it the greatest in the land."

William made his eyes wide, and he nodded slowly, as if he understood. He did not, I am sure, for he is not that clever. But whatever can Father mean? Northumberland's family can never be the greatest in the land. The King's family is the greatest.

## 7th July 1553

The Tower is alive with rumours. Gossip in the city reached the guards on duty at the gates and, once they heard, so did the rest of us. They say the King is dead, but no one seems to know for sure. There has been no proclamation. If he is dead, then Mary must be queen!

## 8th July 1553

It is true. The King is dead. It is a sad day – he was only fifteen.

Sir John Bridges (the Lieutenant of the Tower) has received a letter announcing the death. Edward died two days ago. But I cannot think why the council kept his death secret. People are saying that as he died there was a great storm and hailstones red as blood beat down. I remember a storm for I was delivering a fruit pie to one of Mother's friends, and it was a very watery pie by the time it reached her. I am sure I would have noticed red hail.

# 9th July 1553

The Tower has been a busier place than usual today. Basket upon basket of food has been brought in – every sort of fowl and fruit you can imagine – and the glorious scent of sweetmeats masks even the stink from the river. There are great sweepings and cleanings and the Yeoman Warders are scarcely to be seen, for they are brushing off their best uniforms, and the Guards are polishing their pikes. This makes me think the Queen will visit soon. But which queen? Mary – or Elizabeth? Oh, my heart burns for it to be Elizabeth. Mary is 37, and plain, and sounds dull to me, but Elizabeth! Elizabeth is said to be very clever, with a lively spirit, and she is only nineteen!

Mother asked why I look so cheerful. She suspects that I have been out talking to Tom, but I have not. I swear that I have almost forgotten him. As he has forgotten me.

# 10th July 1553

It is early morning and the air is fresh and cool. I have been woken by so many comings and goings that I think something important must be happening. I hear marching feet, and men's voices. They try to speak quietly, but their words echo within the Tower walls. I burst to know what is afoot, but I cannot go down below, for fear of waking my brothers and angering Sal who, it is true, has little enough sleep. For a long time, I have been picking at the small hole in my roof with a piece of metal I found outside the Mint. If I make it larger, I will have a little daylight in my garret room. Mother says I burn too many candles, and asks, "Do you think I am made of tallow?" This morning's activity has made me work a little harder at the hole, and I have enough light now to write.

# Later

Such a wonderful day this has been – but strange! We have a queen, and I have seen her. We knew we would have one, but her name is not Mary, nor is it Elizabeth. It is Jane – Jane, the Queen. She is only fifteen years old.

What has happened, Father says, is this. King Edward wished our country to stay Protestant, with the monarch as head of the church in England. Therefore, he did not want the papist (that means Catholic) Mary to succeed him. He really disliked the Catholic church so he wrote a device, like a will, declaring that as both Mary and Elizabeth were not born in legal wedlock they must be known as bastards, and so cannot inherit the crown. Instead, he chose the Lady Jane Grey to be his successor. Lady Jane – I should say Queen Jane – is a Protestant. She is the one Sal told me about, the one who married the Duke of Northumberland's son, Guilford Dudley. Northumberland's name has been on many people's lips today, and they do not always speak politely of him. Some think he deliberately married Guilford to Jane, and that this was part of his big plot to put her on the throne and so make Guilford king. Now he will become grander and richer than he is already, so it will not matter to him that he is not liked. A clever plan.

I wonder if Jane is angry that her parents made her marry Guilford. I am sure she is happy to be queen, but I think that if I were in her place of power, I would punish them.

It grows dark, and my candle is but a stump. I have moved my mattress so that the rising sun will shine on to my face. In the morning I will describe the rest of today's happenings.

## 11th July 1553

I have some time before I must rise and help Mother and Sal. Where shall I begin?

The beginning, of course – the beginning of that glorious summer's afternoon. At midday, here at the Tower, a Royal herald proclaimed Jane as queen, but we knew already. Sal went out before eight to buy a sugar cone and said the heralds had been to other places, too, with trumpeters blowing a fanfare. She said (I do not know if this is true) that few people cheered at the new queen's name. I said, "How unkind," but I realize now that I did not cheer, either. Although it was certain that Mary would not be queen,

I had hoped for Elizabeth – my princess. She is, after all, a Protestant like Edward. Mother said most people had never heard of Jane Grey, so why should they cheer her, and anyway, they probably believed that it was Mary's right to be queen. Father told her to hold her tongue.

At half past two, Sal and I ran down to the river to wait for the procession. Mother followed with the boys. She is still not lively. Father waited at the gate with Sir John, the Lieutenant of the Tower, and the other officials.

We waited an age, but when cheering started from the west, we knew the Royal barge was coming. When it appeared, followed by several others, how Sal and I did gape! The glory of it! The ladies and gentlemen, in red and purple and silver and gold, in velvet and brocade – so beautiful! As they turned their heads to see the people, the sun glinted on the jewels in their caps and head-dresses!

And Jane, the Queen – this is what she wore. A green damask skirt, a green and white bodice (absolutely thick with embroidery), a white head-dress encrusted with jewels, and wooden chopines, strapped beneath her shoes to make people think she is taller. I know, because I saw them as she stepped from the barge. She must indeed be very tiny.

As the guns on the wharf fired their salute to the new queen, she walked into the Tower under a canopy held by six fine men, with her mother bearing her train. As she came close, I saw she has freckles, and her hair looks slightly red. Her husband, Guilford Dudley, was dressed in gold and white, and was bowing to all sides, especially to the Queen whenever she spoke. The Yeomen of the Guard carried gilded axes that flashed in the sun.

I must go downstairs now.

## Much later

At last I can finish my account!

Sir John and the other officials – Father, too – greeted the Queen and escorted her to the White Tower, where the Royal apartments are. Sal and I followed, at a distance. How the people stared as the Porter and guards let us pass! All the Lieutenant's servants were in his garden looking out as the procession skirted the Garden Tower. Most people call it the Bloody Tower now, because of a terrible murder that's supposed to have happened there. (Father says the whole place should be called the Bloody Tower. I say that's horrible, but William says he and Father know what goes on.) We followed up the slope of Tower Green to the White Tower which, thanks to our house being so tall and thin, I can see from the hole in my roof.

A noble knelt to present the keys of the Tower to the Queen, for it is her palace now, but the Duke of Northumberland took the keys and handed them to her himself. As he is her father-in-law, and the main reason she is queen, perhaps he thought it was his right.

At dinner, Father told us how, after the Queen had attended worship in St John's chapel at the top of the White Tower, he had been among those who had knelt before her in the presence chamber below. She was seated on the throne, still beneath the canopy, and he kissed her hand. My father!

They brought her the crown jewels (which I have seen and are glorious) but when they went to put the crown on her, Father says she drew back, shaking her head, and said something like, "The crown had never been demanded by me or by anyone in my name." But they kept on and, in the end, she gave in and allowed them just to see if it fitted. Immediately, she went pale, and Father was called to attend her.

I cannot understand it. I would love to wear the crown. It seems that Guilford will not wear one, though. Father said the Queen was stone-faced at talk of having a crown made for her husband. His father, Northumberland, will not be pleased at that!

Something happened at the banquet which followed. Father has not spoken of it to any of us, but I know! Sal has friends in many places – at least she is useful for something! Apparently a letter arrived from the Lady Mary demanding that she be proclaimed queen immediately, because she is the legal heir to the throne. That must have given them all indigestion! Then in the night there was a row in the Queen's apartments between Jane and Guilford. He brought his mother, the Duchess of Northumberland, into it, and the row grew worse. Indeed, the Duchess made to take Guilford away, but Jane ordered them to stay. They had to obey her – she is the queen! The power is all hers from now on.

## 13th July 1553

I have not seen Queen Jane once since she arrived, and nor has Sal. She has kept to her apartments and has only been seen in public at midday dinner. She stays with her ladies, and is visited when her signature is needed on state papers. This is not how I imagined a young queen would behave. If I were in her place, I would have a banquet every day, with music and dancing and masks and jesters, and all around the room would be dozens of dainty sweetmeats in little dishes, with rose petals scattered in between.

## 14th July 1553

There is trouble, and now I know why the Queen keeps to her rooms. The Duke of Northumberland has taken an army into the east of England, and is to bring back the Lady Mary. The longer she is free, they fear, the more people will rally to support her claim to the throne. But it is not just ordinary people who wish for a daughter of Henry VIII to be queen – the gentry do, too, and are refusing to help Northumberland capture her.

## 17th July 1553

This morning, Mother told me to chase after Sal, who had gone to the market. The stupid girl forgot to take any money. I ran out, and as I rounded the Byward Tower I bumped into Tom – really bumped! It was so sudden that we burst out laughing. And he had been coming to look for me, to tell me that in the afternoon a pair of leopards was to arrive.

"Maybe the Queen will wish to see them," he said. I did not think so, but would not spoil his excitement. He walked with me to the gates, which was lucky, because the Tower dog-keeper came up behind us and we were surrounded by his slobbery mastiffs. They were loose, and I do not care for dogs at all, having often been snapped at by the shoemaker's nasty little terrier.

Tom knows I am afraid. "I'll walk alongside of you for a step or two, Tilly," he said, and took my arm, which I liked. As we talked he told me why he has not spoken to me. At first it was because of the baby that died. He felt awkward, he explained, and did not know what to say, so hid his face when he saw me. "And then," he said, "you were cold to me."

"Are you surprised?" I asked, crossly, and we nearly quarrelled again.

As we reached the corner where the one-legged beggar sings his saucy songs, Sal appeared, hot and red-faced. I gave her the money, and told her to be quick, for Mother needed her. She stuck her tongue out at me, but I just gave her a superior sort of smile – I was with Tom after all! Tom and I walked home, and all was peaceful until we reached the Lion Tower. Master Worsley had turned up early, so had the leopards, and Tom was in bad trouble for walking out without permission. I don't know who snarled more, the leopards or Master Worsley. It was time to go!

In the early evening, while Father and William were attending a prisoner in the Martin Tower, Mother dozed beside the fire and I slipped back down to the Lion Tower.

The leopards were in their cage, but were angry and tired all at once, and of course there was no word of the Queen coming. Tom and I talked, and I was telling him all I knew of the problems with the Lady Mary, when suddenly we realized that there were none of the usual comings and goings outside. We strolled towards the Middle Tower and saw the guard party just in the act of locking the gates. I could not believe it – it was far too early. I yelled for them to stop and let me through. It was fortunate that two of the guards know me well, for Father always threatened William and me with a whipping if we should ever be outside the gates at locking-up time. Once the gates are closed, they are opened for no one less than the monarch.

A lucky escape, but I am happy because Tom and I are friends again. I must ask him why he seems to like Sal so much. It still makes no sense to me.

# 18th July 1553

The gates were locked early last night because one of the Queen's council had slipped out, and it was thought he might be up to no good. He was brought back later, but the Queen wanted to make sure nobody else had the same idea. Everyone in the Tower is testy and their nerves trouble them. The news from the Duke of Northumberland is not good, they say. I think that must depend whether you are for the Queen or for the Lady Mary. The crews of six ships, sent to stop Mary escaping the country, have changed sides, and she now has a huge number of supporters and protectors.

"What will happen now?" I asked William.

"I shall not waste words explaining," he said, looking down his sharp nose. "You would not understand."

In my opinion, he does not know. He is a pompous ass.

## Later

Father would not let me stir today, not even as far as Tower Green. There are more men guarding the Tower today than ever before, and many of Queen Jane's nobles have left. Father snaps at everyone, and Mother weeps all over the house. "The poor child," she says. She means the Queen. "God help her."

Never mind the Queen – what about me? I am cooped up like a hen. Father told Mother to keep me busy, so I have been made to cook and sweep and weed, and to feed children and chickens until my legs ache and my hands are red and sore.

## 19th July 1553

God help the Queen. But which queen do I mean? We seem to have two.

This afternoon Tom came to fetch me (and Sal, which

made me cross). "Come into the city!" he said. "The Lady Mary is to be queen!"

Mother would not let Sal go, for someone had to look after Harry and Jack. I remembered then what she did the day before yesterday, and stuck my tongue out at *her*. That pleased me.

As we started off, church bells began to ring from all directions. I looked back over the top of the Lord Lieutenant's lodgings at the turrets of the White Tower and thought about little Queen Jane. How long would she be there?

My candle flickers. I will rise early to write more. Meanwhile, I shall work a little at my hole in the roof. It needs to be bigger. Then I shall sleep – if I can. The bells have not stopped!

## 20th July 1553

It is very early in the morning, and church bells still ring! Yesterday the whole of London was alive with whispers and shouts and talk and cheers and quarrelling. In the late afternoon, the Lord Mayor of London proclaimed the Lady Mary, daughter of the noble King Henry VIII – Queen of England, France and Ireland!

All around us the people went wild! Bells chimed and pealed and there were fires lit in the street, and children danced, though I am sure they could not understand. Tom and I could scarcely hear ourselves speak! He was scared he might lose me in the throng, and held tight to my hand. I liked that.

We made our way – slowly because of the crowds – as far as St Paul's, which must be more than a mile. The name "Mary" was on everybody's lips, and those who spoke for Jane were quickly silenced as the mob closed round them. Tom would not let me stop to see what happened.

Outside every tavern, drunken men and women staggered about laughing and singing. I do not think they were capable of knowing who was queen, but they were good-natured and did not bother us. We passed a man leading a dancing bear and swigging from a tankard. He was clearly very drunk, and was being chased and taunted by a group of children. I was afraid he might let go of the bear, and told the smallest children to stay back, but they cursed me – such words as I have never heard except from soldiers!

At St Paul's there was a great gathering – more people than I have ever seen (except at executions) and even the church bells couldn't drown the noise they made! We did not stay there long. St Paul's churchyard reeks of rotting corpses more than any other I know, and on this warm summer evening, it was worse than ever. Father says the graves are too shallow.

We turned about and made our way back by a different route. While we were watching a juggler who used knives and did not cut himself, Tom said, "It grows dark, Tilly. Do you think they might close the gates early tonight?"

We ran!

"If you are locked out," Tom panted, "you will have to sleep where I do, in the Lion Tower."

I laughed. I have seen where he sleeps. It is little better than the animals' cages, and I think the lion called Edward VI (after the late king) sleeps in more comfort.

## Later

Mother and Sal have gone to the city, William is closeted with Father and his friends downstairs, and the boys are asleep, full of a good dinner. Through the hole in my roof, which is now the size of a large cooking apple, I can see the early afternoon sun lighting the White Tower. Just now, while I put the pots away, I listened to the men's talk. Yesterday, poor Jane – just Lady Jane once more – was told by her own father, the Duke of Suffolk, "You are not the queen any more," and he tore down the canopy of state – tore it down! She was utterly dignified – simply said she was quite happy to give up the crown, and asked to go home. Suffolk, cruel man, leaving her with just her women, went out through the main gates on to Tower Hill and shouted, "God save Queen Mary!" or something similar and disappeared. That is a change of heart (if he has a heart).

Now there are guards at Lady Jane's door. But they are there to keep her in.

Mother has returned. I must stop writing and look as if I am attending to Harry and Jack.

## 21st July 1553

Guilford's father is under guard now, and we expect Queen Mary in London soon. I suppose she will come here. I was going to say that she will be safe, but poor Jane Grey was not. Two days ago she was the queen. Now she is a prisoner, and so is Guilford. My uncle told us that after Jane's father gave her the news and tore down her canopy of state, she said to her old nurse, Mrs Ellen, "I am glad I am no longer queen." Her ladies said nothing. They could not speak for weeping. They fear that the Lady Jane is now in danger of her very life. To take the throne from the true monarch is treason, and the punishment for this is beheading.

Today Father sent William to deliver an ointment to the Master of the Wardrobe. William has no apprentice to make him look important, so he made me carry his bag. I longed to tell the people we passed that there was nothing more in it than a book, a pair of gloves, and some gooseberries, which he is to deliver to the Master's wife. As we passed the White Tower, I looked up. I did not know which were the Lady Jane's windows, and William would not tell me (he does not know, I am sure) but I smiled and hoped she saw me and would know that someone thought kindly of her. She must be so frightened, and when I think of that small freckled face, I want to cry. But I dare not say this aloud. Father warns us every day that the stone walls of the Tower have ears. And so have I! I believe I learn more by being quiet and listening, than by asking questions and getting scolded for being pert.

### 25th July 1553

Our house being against one of the outer walls of the Tower, I can often hear when something is happening on Tower Hill – as long as the rest of the family is quiet. This evening, Father and William have been called away to attend Mistress Partridge, the wife of the Gentleman Gaoler, who has a fever and sweats mightily. We are told to pray that it is not the sweating sickness, or we are all in danger of our lives. I prayed a good deal, but had to stop because I cannot concentrate for wondering what is going on outside the Tower. I can hear shouts, and horses squealing. I wonder if I might slip out of the house without Mother seeing me.

## Later

There is much trouble. As I turned into the lane by the water, towards the Tower gates, I had to jump aside as a strange procession came towards me. Procession is the wrong word, for that implies something grand and beautiful. The men entering the Tower might have been grand last week, but tonight they are prisoners, and a sorry sight. The Duke of Northumberland, who put the Lady Jane on the throne, led his sons and other nobles, surrounded by a larger number of guards than I have ever known before. He held his head high.

It was soon clear that the guards were not there just to prevent Northumberland from escaping. He needed them to protect himself from the angry Londoners. Like the others with him, he was plastered with muck and filth, thrown by the people. I swear my mother could have smelt him from our house. Slimy raw egg hung in strings from his hair, and bits of shell clung to his clothes. His eldest son looked as if he was struggling to hold back tears. Indeed he was, for William told Mother later that as the prisoners were marched past the Garden Tower and they saw Tower Green he began to howl, and wept all the way to the Beauchamp Tower, where they were imprisoned. He howled with terror, I suppose, and I am not surprised, for these men stand accused of the worst crime of all. Treason.

I almost feel sorry for them. If Edward VI wrote that he wished the Protestant Lady Jane to be queen, then is that not the law? But William says that people who wanted to be rich and powerful put Jane on the throne for their own ends, and that is Northumberland's crime. Perhaps he somehow talked Edward into naming Jane as his heir.

It seems Northumberland will be punished – together with all the others involved. I suppose it is right and proper. But I do feel sorry for the Lady Jane. I believe it was never her wish to be queen, so surely she will not be so severely punished.

## 26th July 1553

The Lady Jane, with her three women and her page, is to be moved from the White Tower to the Gentleman Gaoler's lodgings. I am pleased, for Master Partridge is a kind man, and his house is next to the Beauchamp Tower, where Guilford is imprisoned with his father and brothers. I am sure she will be allowed to walk on Tower Green, and maybe Guilford will see her. Perhaps I will, too. She might even speak to me. Imagine – to be addressed by a queen – even one who was queen for only nine days!

## 27th July 1553

Father has forbidden me to wander the Tower as I am used to doing. "There are new warders and guards who do not know you," he said. I will offer to help him and William and Mother whenever they go out of the house. That way, everyone will soon recognize me as the physician's daughter, and I will be able to wander freely as before. And why not? Father's father was once the Tower physician, too, so we are true Tower people, and have every right to be here.

I love to wander. There are many small towers along the outer and inner walls. Some hold prisoners, of course, and give me shivers, but in others I often find someone to talk to, or somewhere cool to sit when it is hot. Some parts of the Tower are far too noisy and busy. The Mint is dreadful. There it is hot and smoky and smelly, and how they manage to turn out such beautiful shining coins from all that busyness, I do not know.

One good thing is that Mother has said I may walk into the city occasionally, but I am not to stop at the menagerie. I promised I would not. Today I spent an hour there, talking with Tom, but I did not break my promise. How? I simply kept walking, and did not stop! There was bear-baiting this morning, and a mastiff had been killed. I followed Tom as he cut chunks of meat from the dead dog and tossed it to the beasts. How they rage and roar and tear at the flesh! I had to leave when a party of ladies and gentlemen wanted to be shown the new monkey. I am furious with Tom. I had not known there was a new one, and when I told Sal she said, "Oh, yes, I know."

"How did you know?" I asked.

"Tom showed it me, he did," she said, and tossed her head. I asked her what it was like, and she said, very slowly, "Well, let me see, 'tis brown, methinks, with spots." I was suspicious, and said, "Tom told me it has long claws shaped like hooks. Is that true?" Sal nodded. "Ay," she said, "'tis true, and I have seen them."

She lies. She has not seen it.

## 30th July 1553

Yesterday, Princess Elizabeth rode into London at the head of 2,000 men all dressed in green and white! William said the colours are to show the people that she, as well as Mary, is a Tudor princess and I think, for once, that he is right. From what I overheard after church this morning, I gather that Elizabeth fears for her own safety. She, like poor Lady Jane, is a Protestant, and there are concerns in Royal circles that she might be planning to seize the throne, to keep England Protestant. She has come to London to show the Queen that she is Her Majesty's true and loyal subject and does not desire the throne. I pray nightly for her safety, and that I might have a chance to give her her mother's precious little letter.

# 31st July 1553

The Lady Jane's father, the Duke of Suffolk, has been a prisoner in the Tower for the last three days, and no one told me. "What need have you to know?" Father demanded. I was about to tell him that I write such things in my diary, but I shut my mouth. I do not think he would approve.

The Duke is a lucky man, but a cruel one. He is lucky because Queen Mary has allowed him to go free. He is cruel because the talk in the Tower is that he has made no attempt to plead for his daughter's freedom. He and his Duchess scuttled away as fast as they could. Mother says it is because he is afraid for his own life, but I still think that he is bad. Even though my father is stern, and not very understanding, I believe he would always try to keep me safe.

I think the Duke will behave himself from now on, because Queen Mary will be watching him. I know I would!

## 2nd August 1553

Princess Elizabeth and her men (fewer this time) have ridden out of London to meet Queen Mary's procession and tomorrow they will ride back into the city, together! And, better than that – the Queen is to lodge here, at the Tower of London! Oh, what a sight we shall see! I hope the Princess Elizabeth will come too.

I keep the letter safely for her.

## 3rd August 1553

This morning, Father and William were out early among the Tower dignitaries – making ready for the Royal arrival! I rose early to do my work, because I wanted so much to be finished in time to watch the Queen and Princess Elizabeth ride into the city. As I worked, I plotted ways to persuade Mother to let me go and see it all for myself. But I need not have worried. Mother said, "This is a great day, Tilly – one you must remember to tell your children. Would you like to watch the procession enter the city?"

I hugged her. "Oh, thank you!" She hugged me back, smiling, then pushed me away. "Hurry and get ready, child!"

It is so good to see her smile again. And Sal was furious because Mother did not suggest she should go. That was good, too.

Tom was not allowed out either. Master Worsley was cautious in case the Royal party wished to see the wild beasts, and all the menagerie workers were busy with buckets of water and shovels.

It did not matter that I was alone. The people were excited and happy, and my only worry was watching out for cutpurses. I had brought money to buy a pie or two, for I would miss dinner.

I made my way to Aldgate, where there were flowers and faces at every window, but could not get near the gate itself for the heaving crowd. It was impossible to see anything, so I climbed on a barrel outside an inn, and looked across people's heads. Trumpeters were posted on each side of the gate, and the Lord Mayor was already waiting, so I guessed the procession would not be long in coming.

In fact it was ages. I grew hungrier and hungrier, but I knew if I got down to buy a pie, somebody else would take my barrel. There was a man close by who looked as if he'd like to knock me off and climb up himself.

49

Just as I thought I might pass out from hunger, faint cheers from beyond the gate told us the Royal party was on its way. In the distance, I saw caps tossed high in the air. Then through the gate came soldiers, their armour and weapons gleaming in the late afternoon sun. The cheers grew louder, and trumpets sounded, so I guessed the Queen must be passing through the gate into the city, but I could still see nothing.

"Will she come this way?" I asked a man who carried his small son on his shoulders. The child's eyes were almost level with mine.

"She might," he replied, "or she might turn down towards Tower Hill."

It was clear I wasn't going to see much from where I was, so off I jumped. I knew where I could get a good view. Two fat boys scrambled for my place and knocked the barrel over. I fought my way through the crowds and – oh, delight – in a narrow alley that runs down towards Tower Hill, I met a pieman who had been to refill his tray. I bought two meat pies, and stuffed one inside my pocket for later. The one I ate was so hot the gravy burned my mouth, but it tasted better than anything I have eaten for months!

I hurried past the guards into the Lion Tower, and raced round shouting for Tom. Master Worsley caught me, but he was in a good mood, and let me go up the steps to the walkway below the battlements to watch the procession. Once he'd gone down to the gates, Tom climbed up beside me.

When the Tower cannons began their thundering salute, we knew the procession was near. Soon we heard the clatter of hooves on cobbles. It echoed as the horses passed beneath the gatehouse, and we cheered as soldiers, nobles and gentlemen passed in all their glory. But if they were brilliant, they were nothing compared with the two shining Royal ladies. The Queen was dressed in purple and gold, so rich it glowed. Princess Elizabeth wore white and I thought she was so beautiful.

I don't know what possessed me. I knelt down and leaned over the edge of the walkway, which is dangerous in itself, and then I did what was, although I did not realize it, a far more dangerous thing. "My Lady!" I shouted. Tom gripped my ankle. "My Lady Elizabeth! I have something for you!" I was annoyed that I hadn't brought the letter with me, but if she would only stop I could tell her about it. Before I knew what was happening, two guards grabbed me by the elbows and pulled me down from the walkway and away from Tom.

My candle is dying. I must wait for sunrise to finish this. Mother said I should remember to tell my children about this day. No need. They will be able to read my diary – maybe!

# 4th August 1553

I am the luckiest person. In the excitement of yesterday, no word reached Father of what happened. When I shouted, I only had eyes for Princess Elizabeth, but Tom told me the Queen herself heard me. He said her head snapped round and she glared up at me, then spoke sharply to a noble at her side. He shouted to a guard, and that was when I suddenly found myself on the ground, my arms grasped so tightly that I fancy I can still feel the hands gripping me.

One of them bellowed at me, but there was so much din from the procession that I couldn't hear. He shouted again. "Answer me, girl! What is it you have for my Lady Elizabeth?"

"N-nothing," I stammered.

"Take a look," he said and, without warning, the other one opened my pocket and thrust his fist inside. If I had not been so frightened, I would have laughed, for his hand came out clutching a broken, dripping pie! He swore, and I wish I had remembered the words he used so I could tell Tom.

"What's that?" the first guard demanded.

I have always been quick with my tongue, and for once my

brain worked at the same speed. "It was a pie, for the Lady," I said. "I thought she might be hungry, and now it is ruined!" I began to sob, most realistically. If they had asked why I did not have a pie for the Queen, I would have said something about how she would not want the people to see her with a meat pie in her hand, but they did not. Instead, they laughed so hard I thought I might laugh, too.

Last night I thanked Almighty God that I had forgotten to take the letter with me.

## Later

I am indeed lucky. Father told tales today of people on the streets who had called for the Lady Elizabeth. "Protestants," William said, nodding and trying to look wise, but he is right for once. People feel very strongly, each about their own beliefs. "There are people who are angry that England will now return to the Catholic faith," Father explained to Mother, but I know she does not care if England is Protestant or Catholic. She says we all worship the same God, and we should be allowed to do it in whatever way we wish. At least, she said that once, but Father was so angry that she will never say it again.

We attend service at St Peter's and, as that is within the walls of the Queen's Tower, our services are as she ordains. I have never heard Father speak against the monarch's wishes – not outside our house – and I do not suppose I ever will.

Some of the Protestants Father spoke of were beaten by the Queen's men, and some were taken away. Father said, "Much blood is going to be shed."

I do not agree. I believe Mary will be a good, kind ruler, for I heard that the first thing she did on entering the Tower was to free some of our Catholic prisoners – important men such as Bishop Gardiner and the Duke of Norfolk (who Father attends quite often, for he is ancient). The Yeoman Warder who told me about it said, "That lady needs all the good Catholics she can get." But from the sound of the crowds today, the whole of England is Catholic once more. Anyway, the Queen will live in the White Tower while things settle down, and we are all safe here.

## 7th August 1553

All seems calm at home, but I think not for long! Mother has hired a girl for the day to help with the pickling. Sal is so busy showing off and letting the poor creature see who is in charge that she gets nothing done. I think sparks will fly soon. I hope so. When Mother is busy with Sal, she leaves me to my own devices. I am excused the task because my head aches and vinegar fumes worsen it. In truth I do not have a headache. 'Twas not really a lie – I almost feel I might get one.

## Later

I walked with Tom by the river. We discussed what we will be doing when we are the same age as the Queen. By then I will have children as old as I am now. Tom says he will be Keeper of the Royal Menagerie. I laughed in his face. "I do not think," I said, "that the great Master Worsley need fear his job will be taken by Tom – the son of John the Carter!"

A rumour flying round the Tower says that the Lady Jane has written to Queen Mary begging for forgiveness. She must be so frightened, for the Queen has only to speak and Jane Grey will be doomed.

## 8th August 1553

The Catholic mass is said several times a day in the Queen's chapel. Mary must be truly devout, and her knees must ache, as mine do on Sundays. Father has been asked to attend her twice, to assist her own physicians, but he will tell us nothing except that she is not as tall and slender as Princess Elizabeth, but dresses magnificently.

While Father and William sat together tonight, I heard them saying that Northumberland will be going on trial for treason at Westminster and it is very likely he will be executed. Sal will be excited – Mother always lets her have the morning off for executions. Father also said that he'd heard that the Queen will probably not condemn Jane.

## 18th August 1553

The Duke of Northumberland has been found guilty and, as a traitor, has been sentenced to be hanged, drawn and quartered, and to have his heart taken out of his body and flung in his face. The crowds love that kind of thing, but personally I think it's disgusting. I was pleased that the Queen has been merciful and he is simply to be beheaded in three days' time. I expect we shall all go.

## 21st August 1553

No execution. I don't know why.

## 22nd August 1553

Execution day after all. I've found out it was delayed because Northumberland decided to give up being a Protestant and become Catholic. Perhaps he thought this might soften the Queen's heart, but it's had little effect. She did allow him a day to attend mass to do it, though.

We got to the execution site on Tower Hill quite early. Mother brought the boys because there is a special place where Tower people may stand, which is reasonably safe.

That is just as well, for there were thousands and thousands of people waiting to see the traitor die. And the racket! There were jugglers and minstrels and sellers of fruit and pies and ale. We did not buy anything because Sal and I carried a basket of food between us. I know there were pickpockets and cutpurses in the crowd, for every so often, a fight broke out to cries of "Thief!" Jack pointed to a beggar who frothed at the mouth. "Poor man," he said. I laughed as the crowd chased him away, and told Jack the beggar was a cheat, who ate soap to make himself froth!

We had to wait until Northumberland had been to mass and prayed for his soul, and the boys grew cross. It was a warm day, and they were hot and sticky. And the poor creatures could see nothing but skirts and breeches, except when big Geoffrey from the smithy sat Jack on his shoulders.

When the prisoner appeared the crowd grew so angry that the soldiers had to keep them back by jabbing at them with the pointed ends of their halberds. As the Duke climbed the scaffold steps, the shouts of anger turned to demands for the executioner to get on with it and finish off the traitor.

He prayed and made his speech – my, he did go on! Then he knelt on the straw and was blindfolded. He still muttered, and the blindfold slipped. He got up, it was retied, he knelt again and put his head on the block.

The executioner limped forwards and raised his axe. Northumberland stretched out his arms and – chop! It was done. The executioner gripped the head by the hair and held it high, blood dripping on his white apron. I swear I saw the lips and eyes move. The head was shown at the four corners of the scaffold, and the executioner shouted, "Behold the head of the traitor!"

The crowd went wild and fought forwards, wanting to dip bits of cloth in the blood that seeped through the boards of the scaffold. I did this at another execution once, with my kerchief, but some blood dripped on my head, which was disgusting, and has quite put me off.

I used the kerchief to try to heal a horrible wart on my finger, but it did not work, and I had to let Father lay mouse flesh on it instead. Ugh.

I wanted to stay on and watch for a while, but Mother said no, there was dinner to get ready and I could keep the boys amused at home.

We followed the body as it was taken into St Peter's to be buried. I suppose the head went to London Bridge, to be stuck on a spike as a warning to anyone else who fancied they might commit treason.

It has just occurred to me that Guilford must have heard the crowds today – must have known that the final mighty cheer was in celebration of the death of his father.

## 28th August 1553

When Bishop Gardiner, who was freed by Queen Mary earlier this month, was imprisoned here, Father attended him so often that they became quite friendly. Now Gardiner has been appointed Lord Chancellor of England, so Father is feeling very important! I think it has given him dreams of becoming a Court Physician, although he does not say so. It is what I would dream in his place.

## 31st August 1553

All the talk is of how Lady Jane has been told that she and Guilford will stand trial, but she must not worry. She will, of course, be found guilty, but is assured that a royal pardon will follow straight away.

Someone from the Mint – Master Lea, I think – dined at Master Partridge's the other night, and Lady Jane was there. From what Master Lea has said (and gossip goes round the Tower very fast these days), she is very different to most fifteen year olds. She is powerfully strong in her faith – she will not become a Catholic – and fixed in most of her opinions. She expressed loyalty to the Queen, which I think is sensible, and she was not complimentary to the dead Duke. I should think not. He, along with Jane's parents, has brought her to the state she is in now. She is, however, far more comfortable than many Tower prisoners. Two of them, Mr Man and Mr Gardiner (not the Bishop!), whose crime was stealing hawks, are to be put to torture as an example to others. That does not seem as bad to me as treason, and yet Lady Jane, who will be tried for treason, dines with the Gentleman Gaoler.

## 7th September 1553

Our birthday (Princess Elizabeth and me). I am now thirteen years old, and Elizabeth is twenty. By the time she was my age, her father had remarried four times and she was with her fourth stepmother, Katherine Parr.

## 14th September 1553

I am not allowed to move about alone at the moment. One after the other, important prisoners are being brought into the Tower, and Father says I should stay out of the way. I thought all this would be over once Mary was queen, but as some are freed, others are imprisoned. Catholic out – Protestant in. Today the Archbishop of Canterbury, Thomas Cranmer, who has talked too loudly against the Catholic mass, was brought in. He is being kept in the Garden Tower, which is not so bad, as he is almost sure to be allowed to walk in the Lieutenant's garden. It's much nicer than ours, which is all beans and onions and cabbages.

## 27th September 1553

The Queen is back here for the last few days before her coronation. Princess Elizabeth is here, too. I heard them arrive, but did not see them, for Mother has said that if I wish to watch the coronation procession, I must keep up with my housework and mend my best cap.

They say that Mary keeps a close eye on Elizabeth. She is still a Protestant, although Mary is trying to make her change.

I have taken out the Princess's little letter from its hiding place, just to look at it. I even went down to dinner with it in my pocket, but I felt all hot, and almost guilty when Father came in. William asked if I had a secret, and started teasing me about Tom, which made Mother absolutely wild. Not with William – with me!

## 29th September 1553

The Queen will leave tomorrow for Whitehall, ready for her coronation. Father says I must stay on Tower Hill with the rest of the family and watch the procession leave. I begged to be allowed to go into the city, to be among the crowds, which would be much more exciting, but he said no, I am a young woman now and must be protected from unsavoury characters. I said Tom would protect me, but all that did was earn me a swipe from Mother. She missed, but did Sal gloat! I met Tom this morning anyway, when I took swill down for the pigs, and he cannot go tomorrow either because someone must stay with the beasts, and he is the lowest. He does not mind, as he will watch the procession leave. I remembered the day I stood on the wall and shouted for the Princess. That I will not do tomorrow. But, one day, I will find a way to give her the letter. If I could be sure she would be in no danger, I would simply send it to her with her page, who I see often around the Tower. I do not know what is in the letter, but I do know that her mother was known by all sorts of names, such as the Protestant Witch (and worse, William told me once, but he will not say what).

Suppose the letter said something like, "If Mary gets the throne, take it from her"? If it were found, it would be a death sentence for Elizabeth. And it would have been my fault.

All this thinking gives me a headache.

## 30th September 1553

I could not go to Tower Hill today as I was taken ill last night. My head has been so sore, and I am still hot. Father says there is nothing much wrong. I wish he had my head. He would be sorry then.

Tom sneaked in while the family were on Tower Hill, to tell me what he saw as the procession left. He twittered on about soldiers and armour and weapons until I wanted to slap him. "Tell me about the ladies," I said. "There were many," he said, "all finely dressed." He also told me that Princess Elizabeth rode with one of her stepmothers, Anne of Cleves, and that the Queen wore a head-dress that shone like a crown. Not enough detail for my liking! Then he carried on about how the Master of the Horse had nodded to him, which is rot.

Sal said that an acrobat balanced on the spire of St Paul's. Can that be true? You can never tell with Sal. I should like to have seen it myself.

## 1st October, 1553

Today the Queen is being crowned by Bishop Gardiner (who cannot be such a good friend of Father, as he did not invite him to the coronation) in Westminster Abbey. There is to be a great feast afterwards.

I wonder how Lady Jane Grey feels.

## 2nd October 1553

Father came up to my little room to see how I am. He was kind, but not all that sympathetic. When he told me he would send Sal up with one of his disgusting medicines, I threw myself over in bed, and my diary fell to the floor. "Ah, the book," he said, and opened the front cover. "I must read it when I have time – find out how my little girl sees her life." I was horrified, but dared not let him see how I felt, in case he thought I had something to hide. I slid my book gently from his hands, and took the opportunity to ask again who gave it to him. "A lady," he said, "just a lady." And climbed back down the ladder. He paused at the foot of the steps and I heard him sigh, "A lady who lost her head because she angered a king." There! Does that not prove she was Anne Boleyn? The letter must be for Princess Elizabeth.

I am going to hide my diary behind the beam above my roof hole, with the letter. It will be very inconvenient, as it is quite an effort to reach it, but that's better than risking anyone finding it. I shall take out my diary only when Father and William are out or asleep. I do not fear Mother coming up here, and Sal only puts her head through the hatch. I have forbidden her ever to set one foot up here. If she does, I will get her into such trouble, and she knows it.

## 15th October 1553

Church is very different now, and I do like the statues and pictures and the beautiful stained glass windows. Looking at them helps pass the time, especially now it is colder. Sometimes my feet are so icy from the chill stone floor that they will hardly carry me out of St Peter's. It is forbidden to say you don't like the Catholic mass, or you do not believe in it, and we no longer use our Book of Common Prayer, which is a shame. It was easy to understand, unlike the new Latin services – they are impossible to follow and make me sleepy. Father says I can still talk to God at my nightly prayers in the way I am used to doing. But he seems troubled and says that not everyone will find it easy.

I was sitting out of the wind in a sunny corner today, watching the ravens and eating apples. Some Tower men strolled past and did not notice me. When I heard the

Queen's name mentioned, I stopped crunching and listened. They spoke of her marrying and said that she needs an heir to the throne. I cannot believe she is thinking of having a first child – she will be all of 38 in the spring.

## 10th November 1553

Today I saw Guilford Dudley walking with his brothers, high on the battlements of the Beauchamp Tower. It would be so wonderful if the Lady Jane was walking on the green, and looked up to see him. She cannot love him – after all she was forced to wed him – but they must have become friends. And if I were in her shoes, having any sort of friend about me would be a comfort. Any prisoner in the Tower of London must feel in danger until he or she walks out through the gates – without a guard.

Lady Jane and Guilford are to go on trial on Tuesday. Perhaps they will be able to talk to each other on the way to the Guildhall. Archbishop Cranmer and some of Guilford's brothers will be on trial, too. I am going down to the river to watch them leave. My mother thinks that Lady Jane will lose her life, but the Queen has promised she will not, Father says. When he had left to treat Master Partridge's wife for what he calls her "interminable aches", Mother muttered, "King Henry was known to break promises, so why should his daughter be any different?"

## 14th November 1553

Mother has been out helping one of her friends who is ill after the birth of a baby. I admire her for doing that, as it is not long since – I was going to say since her own baby died, but I find myself wanting to say "my sister". Susannah.

The trial is over. I did not see them leave – Mother knew what I was up to when I offered to go out early to buy the fish, so she sent Sal. Well, Sal saw nothing either. Halberdiers were everywhere, and they turned her away when she tried to go down to see the barge.

However, I did manage to be sitting on a step in front of the Long House of Ordnance when the Lady Jane, her husband and the other prisoners were brought back from their trial. Someone in the escort always carries an axe, and if the edge is turned away from the prisoner, he or she will live, so that is what I was keen to see. But no. The axe was turned towards the prisoners.

The Lady Jane looked even smaller than before, now she was without her finery or chopines on her feet. She wore black and carried what looked like a prayer book – it was hard to see at that distance, but she is so devout that I am sure I am right. She was unable to speak to Guilford Dudley, for they were separated by guards. How cruel. Imagine being sentenced to death when you are barely sixteen. I wonder whether Guilford will be pardoned?

## 17th November 1553

The Lady Jane was sentenced to be burned alive or beheaded, and the Archbishop, Guilford and his brothers were sentenced to be hanged, drawn and quartered.

## Later

I am taking a chance in writing my diary now for William is thundering about downstairs, angry because Father shouted at him in front of Sal. He mixed some potion or other and got it wrong, and the poor patient was sicker than ever. Father's potions always make me feel sick, even when he makes them. They are usually bitter.

Heard that the Queen is to marry a Catholic prince of Spain. He is Philip, the son of the Holy Roman Emperor, Charles V. I find this so strange as she has never seen him – not even a portrait.

## 25th December 1553, Christmas Day

I think Mother is with child again. After church today Father told me that she will need much more help than usual. That makes me cross, because I help as much as I possibly can, and I am afraid that this time Mother, not the baby, will die. It has made me realize that although I often find her unkind, I truly do love her. Sal does not know yet, but William does. He tries to act in a doctorly way with Mother, but he looks so foolish. I hope Father never lets William try to cure me of anything.

Princess Elizabeth has left London, so there is no chance of giving her the letter now, but I am sure she will return for the Queen's marriage. Perhaps she will come to the Tower again then.

I glimpsed Lady Jane in the Lieutenant's garden. She was well wrapped up against the bitter cold and wore mittens and held a small book, which was probably her prayer book. Father says she is allowed other books, and may walk outside the Tower under guard, so she is not uncomfortable. He knows this because Lady Jane has frequently been unwell recently, and Father has attended her. I think I would be ill if I were cooped up for too long.

## 1st January 1554

The start of another year. We began the last with a Protestant king, and we begin this with a Catholic queen who will marry soon and produce an heir for England.

Tom tells me that Lady Jane will be kept here until Queen Mary has her first child and the succession is safe. He speaks sense sometimes, although he is only a beast keeper. One of Mistress Partridge's maids told Sal that Lady Jane is only allowed to walk in the Lieutenant's garden now. She is probably better off inside – it's so cold in the gardens with the snow lying thick on the ground.

# 3rd January 1554

Yesterday I was dozing (instead of sewing) in front of the fire when I was woken by the sound of gunfire thundering round the Tower walls. I dashed outside and found it was a salute to a great party of Spaniards, newly arrived, with marriage papers for the Queen to sign. They also carried chests full of gifts. Lucky Mary – all I received when I went back to the house was a boxed ear for leaving the boys unattended.

The marriage to Prince Philip grows nearer, but there are people who wish to remove Mary from the throne before it can take place. I suppose they are afraid that Spain will get a hold on our country, and rule us. I wonder who these rebels would put on the throne if they succeeded in removing the Queen. The Lady Jane? Princess Elizabeth? If the Queen knows of this, which I am sure she does, I would not wish to be in either of those ladies' shoes.

Father says there will be blood spilt in the Tower before this is over. That will be nothing new – the Tower is a bloody place. They think I do not know what goes on in the dungeons, or in the cellars of the White Tower, where walls are so thick no screams can be heard. They think I do not know of the place called Little Ease, so tall and narrow that prisoners can barely sit, and can never lie down. William once delighted to tell me of such things, but now he is far too important to bother with me, strutting around like a black crow, carrying Father's medicine chest.

## 14th January 1554

Queen Mary has overcome any plans the rebels might have to prevent her marriage to Philip of Spain. The marriage treaty was signed two days ago, so that is that. When I told William this, he said, "You speak rot. Girls know nothing of such matters, and if you had an ounce of sense you would realize that signing a piece of paper does not make angry men content." He is a pig.

## 27th January 1554

I simply have to write in my diary tonight, even though Father is in the house, for William was right. There is an uprising. A man called Sir Thomas Wyatt has gathered an army of men and occupies the town of Rochester, in Kent. They are not just ordinary men – he even has the crews of royal ships on his side, and many Londoners are shouting for him, too.

Apparently Lady Jane's father, the Duke of Suffolk, is supporting Wyatt. That must mean they intend to put her on the throne a second time. This is like a war, and Wyatt will come to London. I know what that will mean. "Matilda, do not set foot outside the Tower walls." I shall just have to keep out of Father's way, so I do not hear those words. If I do not hear them, I cannot disobey them!

## Later

My big ears have discovered that Sir Thomas Wyatt is the son of a poet who once admired Princess Elizabeth's mother, Anne Boleyn. Maybe he wants to put Princess Elizabeth on the throne instead. I could have a letter for our future queen – how exciting!

## 2nd February 1554

I have no need to be told not to stir outside the Tower. This is the safest place in London and I am glad to be here. While she was out shopping in the city, Mother heard that Wyatt was marching towards London, right this minute, with an army of more than 50,000 men! London Bridge and all the city gates are being strongly guarded. She hurried home as fast as she could (considering her condition) and says she is not leaving these walls until all is peaceful.

Sal started sobbing. "Oh, please'm," she cried, "don't send me out to market, the soldiers might kill me." Mother looked at her crossly and said, "Get on with those parsnips, you silly creature," and I said, "Goodness, Sal, what a fuss you do make," and she glared at me through her tears. All she has done since is lurk in corners, looking whey-faced.

In truth, I do not blame her for being afraid.

## 3rd February 1554

I keep my diary beneath my pillow again, for everyone is so busy that it is quite safe. If Wyatt comes to London, he is sure of a good fight, because the Queen made such a rousing speech that she now has thousands and thousands more people on her side. So let him come! The Tower guns are ready, for through my roof hole I have seen ammunition being wheeled from the Long House of Ordnance down to the Water Gate, so the soldiers are well prepared.

## Later

The Yeoman Warders are really angry! They have heard that Wyatt is demanding that the Queen should surrender her throne and the Tower! Ridiculous – no one can take this place from the people who love it, and that means all of us who live here. Wyatt and his rebels are camped across the river, and the whole of London is ready for battle.

Sal heard that poor Tom was sent to buy meat for the beasts and was unable to find any, for all shops and market stalls are shut up, and the streets are quiet and still. He has to hunt for rats instead.

## 4th February 1554

All that talk of 50,000 rebels was just tittle-tattle! Wyatt had scarcely more than 3,000 men, a Chief Yeoman Warder said. We are well guarded. There is nothing to worry about. But I know one person who must be crazed with fear – Lady Jane Grey. If Wyatt should not succeed, then surely her father, Suffolk, will be put to death. He has been a wicked, unfeeling father to her, I know, but she must care something for him. This is a bad time for her. Father says she keeps to her rooms, and I do not blame her. She has not yet been pardoned.

## 6th February 1554

The city is safe! Wyatt has gone. There is now no sign of his men on the south side of the river, so it is all over. The sight of the Tower of London with cannons lined up on the wharf, and our strong, determined soldiers ready to defend us, must be enough to scare anybody. The Tower has been here for nearly 500 years and will, I hope, be here for 500 more. By then the city will be bigger, as even now there are so many people coming in from the country to live here. And perhaps more people will have houses of their own, who knows?

## 7th February 1554

We were wrong in thinking we were safe. Wyatt had not returned to Kent. He went west and crossed the river on the other side of London. Then he marched his men, who were rather tired and hungry, into London early this morning.

There was much fighting with the Queen's men on the way, first at St James's, and then at Charing Cross. We could hear it from here! By then, Wyatt did not have so many supporters, as lots had deserted. The Chief Yeoman Warder had reports of fighting and terror at Whitehall Palace.

It must be so hard to be queen when you are threatened by others, for you must appear to be strong, so that others around you do not lose heart and flee. And Mary was strong, for she ordered everyone to start praying. God certainly answered their prayers, because Wyatt gave himself up not long afterwards, and just two hours ago, he arrived here in the Tower! Not in the way he imagined, of course, but cold, tired, and miserable. One of the soldiers who handed him to the Tower guards had a slight arrow wound in his leg, and Father was called to tend him. Sal, as usual, went white at the sight of the blood on Father's cuff, so I had to scrub it, but that is how I heard all the news and how I know that Wyatt is in the Bell Tower. He will not sleep tonight. If I know the warders, they will make sure he doesn't. A man who threatens to invade the Tower is not a welcome guest!

## 8th February 1554

There is no pardon for Lady Jane.

## 9th February 1554

Lady Jane Grey and Guilford Dudley should be executed today. But I do not feel sad – because they are still alive! The date has been changed to the 12th.

Guilford will certainly die, but there is still hope for Lady Jane. Queen Mary has been merciful, and yesterday sent her own confessor, Doctor Feckenham, whom Father knows well, to reason with her and to get her to renounce her faith and become a Catholic. As I see it, if she does change, the Protestants will no longer wish to put her on the throne, so she will not be a threat to Mary. Changing will surely be no problem. She is not, after all, being asked to give up God.

## 10th February 1554

Doctor Feckenham is still with Lady Jane. There is no news.

## 11th February 1554

Doctor Feckenham visited Father today. He looks exhausted and aged, although he is not quite as old as Father. I sat by the window with some breeches I am mending for William, who is as careless with his clothes now as he was when he was a boy playing round the workshops and stables. I listened carefully, and this is what I discovered. Suffolk has been captured and brought to the Tower. He was discovered hiding in a hollow tree! What a ridiculous way to behave, when I remember that he was for nine days the father of the queen. He will surely die, Doctor Feckenham said, and is in such a poor state that Father may be visiting him soon.

It became difficult for me to hear the conversation then, for Doctor Feckenham dropped his voice as he spoke of his talks with Lady Jane. Luckily, Father called for more wine, and I poured it very slowly and carefully, and could hear much better. It seems Lady Jane will not change her faith. She debated her beliefs with Doctor Feckenham, and was solid and resolved and would not be moved. He will not give up either, he says, and is to visit her again tonight. Then I realized with a shock that the good Doctor is not here to save Jane's life. The Queen sent him to save her soul. Mary sees Jane as a heretic – someone of the wrong faith. So, come what may, the execution will take place tomorrow. Poor, poor Jane.

## 12th February 1554

Through my roof hole I am watching the final touches being put to the scaffold on Tower Green. It is draped in black, and straw has already been strewn around the block to catch the blood. There is no axe yet. The executioner will bring that. I wonder if Mother will let us watch. We usually do, on Tower Hill, but this is the first execution within the Tower walls since I was about one and a half years old. Mother says that was a double execution – a queen and her lady – and tomorrow is the twelfth anniversary of those deaths. I do not remember them, of course, but I will certainly remember this. There have only been five executions on Tower Green, but there have been many, many deaths in other parts of the Tower – some we never hear about. This bloody Tower.

## Later

I have watched a young girl die, and I have made a new friend, both on the same day! We ordinary Tower people weren't allowed near the scaffold – we're not important enough – but we stood against the walls and towers around the edge of the Green. I could have watched from my garret, but I would have heard nothing. I stood with Sal next to the entrance to the Beauchamp Tower, where Guilford Dudley was imprisoned. He was to be executed first, but on Tower Hill. We would miss that, so we thought we'd try to get a good view of him as he came out.

It was mid-morning when the guards fetched him. Everyone fell quiet as he came up the steps on to the Green. I clearly heard him mutter to his companions, "Pray for me, oh, pray for me." As he was led away I glanced at the windows of Lady Jane's lodgings. I wondered if she was watching and how it must feel to watch her husband go to his death, knowing that she would shortly go to hers.

It seemed no time at all before Guilford's covered body, dumped on a cart, was wheeled back into the Tower and up to the Chapel of St Peter's. His head lay apart from his body, wrapped in a bloody cloth.

Sal suddenly leaned forward and looked past me, a stupid grin spreading over her face. I turned to see what she was looking at. It was Tom.

"I saw it happen," he panted. "I thought if I were quick I could get back in time to see this'n, too."

"How did he die?" I asked.

Tom held out one hand palm up, and chopped the other one down sharply across it. "Like that."

Stupid fool. "No, did he die well, like a gentleman?" I asked. Tom told us Guilford's speech was short, then he knelt to pray and "howled his eyes out". Mercifully, his head was taken off with one blow.

A woman nearby hushed us, and pointed. Coming up the slope towards us was the tiny, black-clad figure of Lady Jane Grey, dark against the grass. She read from a little prayer book – I had hardly ever seen her without – and her lips moved slightly as she walked. Her women followed, weeping.

She mounted the scaffold so bravely, and I clearly heard her first words. "Good people, I am come hither to die, and by a law I am condemned to the same. The fact, indeed, against the Queen's highness was unlawful, and the consenting thereunto by me. . ." I heard little more, for I was sobbing myself by then. I don't know why. I have never cried at an execution in my life – she just looked so sad and alone. And none of it was her doing. It was all caused by scheming men (and her horrible mother), greedy for power and riches.

I could scarcely see through my tears, and was much comforted when I felt a strong arm around my shoulders. I leaned into it, and there was no guessing who it was for I could smell him. I wiped my eyes and glanced sideways at Sal. She looked as if she could have battered my brains in, which was also a comfort to me.

The Lady Jane had finished talking. She gave her gloves and kerchief to her woman, and her book to the Lieutenant, who must have been good to her for her to do this. Then she stood for a moment, still, as if she was savouring her last moments on God's Earth. A gust of wind blew the smell of the river across the Green. It must have smelt like freedom.

After the executioner had knelt to ask her forgiveness, Lady Jane knelt, too, on the straw and spoke to him. At dinner Father told us that she said, "Will you take it off before I lay me down?" and he replied, "No, madam." She meant her head.

She tied a cloth around her eyes and reached for the block. It was horrible. The poor girl could not find it, and even where we were, we heard her cry, "What shall I do? Where is it?" A woman nearby muttered, "Help her, someone."

Someone did indeed help, guiding her hands to the block. The only sound to be heard was quiet weeping. Jane laid down her head, spoke a few final words of prayer and – it was done.

So much blood.

There was a hush as I have never heard before – if that makes sense – and then, once more, only weeping, as the tiny body was lifted down to join her husband's for burial in St Peter's. Father came across and took my hands. "Such a little neck," he murmured. "They are always such little necks."

I have tears in my eyes again now, and the candlelight seen through them makes stars, so I cannot see to write.

## 13th February 1554

I feel better today and must write about my new friend. When Tom saw Father coming yesterday, he darted off, closely followed, I might add, by Sal, much to my annoyance. As Father walked me back to our house, we were joined by Master Lea, from the Mint, who said,

"I should like your daughter to meet my niece, newly arrived from Chelsea. They are of a similar age."

Father said, "Matilda would be happy to make your niece's acquaintance." Huh, I thought, Matilda would not. Who wants to have to make conversation with a country bumpkin, and talk of nothing but cows and hay?

I could not have been more wrong! Frances Lea is the greatest of good company. She makes me laugh until I cry, which was most welcome yesterday. I have permission from Father to spend the whole of today acquainting her with the Tower. This has made Mother cross, because I am supposed to sweep my room, which I have not done since early last summer, and she says it is disgusting. Better still, it has made Sal furious. I will hide my book carefully this morning, in case she decides to come up and make mischief.


## 14th February 1554


Such good times yesterday. Frances now knows everybody there is to know in the Tower and, being much more forward than I, is likely to be of great use, for she can talk her way into anything. I just hope she can talk her way out of anything, too! Both Mother and Father are doubtful about her being a suitable friend, but she charms them, too, and as Mother said, "She is a far superior friend for you than that stinking boy Tom." They'll never understand all the things I like about Tom – the way he listens to me, and is all consideration and gentleness – and it's just not worth arguing with them about it. I wonder what Frances will think when she meets Tom. If I decide she can meet Tom. The last thing I want is another rival for his friendship!

The news this evening is that Princess Elizabeth is being brought to London by Queen Mary. I hope they do not think Wyatt's rebellion was anything to do with her. On the other hand, if they do think that, she will surely come to the Tower, and I may see her. Seeing the Lady Jane give her prayer book to a gentleman yesterday reminded me of my book.

On close inspection it is clear that some pages have been carefully cut from the beginning of the book, but I have found some writing! Scratched out, it is true, perhaps by a needle, but there is enough to see that there are two letters. There is an A. The second is less clear, and at first I thought it to be R, but now I am sure it is B. AB, the initials of Anne Boleyn!

My heart aches a little. I see now that the ink on the letter was smudged by the Queen's tears as they fell on the last word she ever wrote to her darling little daughter.

## 17th February 1554

Mother told me today that she is with child. Does she think
I am blind?

## 23rd February 1554

Lady Jane's father, the Duke of Suffolk, was beheaded on
Tower Hill today. Frances, Sal and I went, but it was a cold
day and a dull occasion. There have been many executions
in London since the rebellion, and people cannot always
spare the time from their work to attend the spectacles.
They say that London Bridge has never been adorned with
so many heads on spikes as these last two weeks. At least the
high Tower walls keep the worst of the wind from us, which
could bring the stench right in. I shall go to see them when
the weather is warmer, as it is only half a mile away. Queen
Mary has ordered that the bodies of all the traitorous rebels
should be hung where people can see them. It's lucky it is

cold just now – it is surprising how little time it takes for flesh to rot and become infested with maggots, which is a revolting sight.

I hear that Princess Elizabeth has only just reached Whitehall Palace. The journey took so long because she is not well at present.

"It is likely the Lady Elizabeth may not live to share her next birthday with you, Tilly," William told me. "The talk is that she was involved with Wyatt. Dangerous work for one so near the throne. The Queen will not tolerate it."

For once he speaks sense.

## 26th February 1554

Father attended Thomas Wyatt, as he is not sleeping. This is hardly surprising as his life is surely in the greatest danger, and he is being questioned daily. From what Father hints at, these meetings are painful and prolonged. Frances says she believes he is being tortured. I do not like to think of such things. Mother is tired and asked me to wait up to give Father his supper, so I listened carefully when he talked with William over his ham and bread. "Wyatt insists the Lady Elizabeth was not part of his rebellion," he said.

"But he did write to her?" asked William.

"It seems so."

"Undoubtedly, he asked her to join him in restoring a Protestant monarch – herself – to the throne," William said, his silly head nodding wisely (he thinks).

"Do not repeat those words outside these walls, boy," Father answered sternly (which made me worry about my loose talk to Frances). "We do not know what the letter said, and he himself insists that the Lady Elizabeth did not write back. She simply said she would do as she should see cause."

Clever Elizabeth! She will be no man's puppet.

## 12th March 1554

I am so busy that I have come to bed exhausted and have not had the energy to reach up for my book until now. Mother says my work is being done well, and she now allows me more time to spend as I wish, as long as I do not go near "the dung-shoveller". I work well to help Mother. I so want both her and this baby to live, but I also work well so that I may meet with Frances. I still see Tom around the Tower, but he is being worked harder and harder and has less time for me now, just as I have less time for him. He and Frances have had few chances to meet so far, and she shows no regret about this.

Frances and I do many things together, but when Father asks what we have been doing, I find it hard to say. "We walk and talk," I begin, and he says, "What do you talk about?" and I reply, "Nothing in particular." And so it is, but we seem to talk about nothing in particular for hours!

After Suffolk's beheading the other week, we were given permission to walk into the city. Sal had to return to the house to attend to the boys, which left Frances and me alone to explore – her first real visit to the city outside the Tower walls. She was amazed at how the houses "huddle together" as she put it. It seems that in the country there is space and grass to spare, and cottages stand apart from each other. She says London is noisy and it stinks. I think the country must stink equally, for everyone there keeps pigs and cows which, as all the world knows, would fill the land with dung if there were not people like Tom to clear it away.

Frances wanted to stop and look at almost every shop or stall we passed, and was surprised at how many there are. She was a little afraid because there were so many people, and thought them most unfriendly. "In Chelsea," she said, "everyone knows everyone else."

"Like in the Tower," I replied, for if the Tower is not just like a village, I do not know what is.

A lad of about our age sauntered past and grinned at us.

Frances smiled back, but I poked her in the ribs and frowned at her, for he looked like a common rascal to me. As indeed he was, for next second, he plunged his hands into an egg-woman's basket, and pulled out two in each hand.

"Thief!" she cried. "Thief!"

Frances stared open-mouthed as the boy took a few steps backwards and waved the eggs in the air, his grin bigger than ever. "He seems to be taunting the old woman," she said.

As it turned out, that is exactly what he was doing. Other stall-holders and shopkeepers came to see what the egg-woman was shrieking about, saw the lad and gave chase. Then did he run! And as soon as they had all turned a corner, a great gang of boys tore through the street grabbing at anything they could lay their hands on from the untended stalls. An upended basket was turned over and a goose escaped and chased after the boys, trying to peck their heels!

We laughed at the cheek of the boys, and wandered through the streets, never too far from the Tower, though. Frances found it hard to keep her feet out of the muck on the floor and keep her eye on windows above. It was only my quickness that saved her twice from being drenched by someone's watery slops.

We grew tired and hungry, and went back to my house for a bowl of pottage, which she pronounced the best she had ever tasted.

"Good," I said. "I made it."

That surprised her, I could see. Sal must have told her I am a bad cook.

The news at home was that the Queen is now formally betrothed to Philip of Spain, which will infuriate Thomas Wyatt, should he hear about it. I am sure he will, for the warders will delight in telling him.


# 17th March 1554


My wish has come true but I pray that God and Princess Elizabeth know that it is not in the way I would want. For a barge has been sent to bring her here, to become a prisoner in the Tower! I am slightly annoyed that I discovered this from Frances, but I am excited that I may be able to see the Princess – if she is allowed to walk about, there will surely now be an opportunity to give her the letter. I offered to take Harry and Jack out to chase the ravens (I did not say that exactly), and spent much of the afternoon wandering past the privy gate, where the steps lead down into the water. She has not arrived, but Frances says she will be here tomorrow. I hope Frances is not full of wild fancies, like Sal.

I am not pleased with Sal, for she told Mother I let the

boys too near the water. I don't know why Mother believes everything Sal says, and takes her word against mine. It was true this time, though.

## 18th March 1554

Such excitement! At this very moment, Princess Elizabeth is dining with the Lieutenant in his lodgings. Only the warders and Tower dignitaries were allowed to watch her arrival, and they all tell different stories, but everyone says she is proud and dignified. I admire that lady so much, I cannot put it into words.

I brought Frances up to my room, which she said was plain but she understood why I liked it. "I have little privacy with my aunt in and out all the time, fussing," she said.

We took turns at the roof hole to look out through the rain to see if we could see the Princess, but we did not. When we went downstairs I asked Mother if I might walk back a little way with Frances. The answer was no, but Frances begged her, "Please! I am still new to the Tower and afraid to walk alone." She put her head on one side and Mother said, "Oh, very well, but be back in an instant, Tilly." We ran off and asked the first Yeoman Warder we met what had happened.

"Poor lady was frightened," he said. "She announced to all who would listen that she is as true a subject of the Queen as anyone now living. Some of the warders felt so bad about what we had to do that they knelt before her."

"Did you?" Frances asked.

"What do you think?" he said. "If Queen Mary, God bless her, does not give England an heir, the Lady Elizabeth might one day be our queen."

Frances whispered to me, "He did."

The warder gazed across Tower Green, to where Lady Jane's scaffold still stood. "She is right to be frightened."

He spoke truth, I told Frances. "Princess Elizabeth's own mother entered the Tower as a prisoner, and never left."

Her eyes widened. "Never? Then where is she?"

I put my lips close to her ear. "Under the floor of St Peter's."

Frances turned green and looked down at the ground.


## 3rd April 1554


I hate Frances Lea! I thank God that I never confided in her about the letter. She has betrayed my trust.

I noticed that Princess Elizabeth walks daily, high up along the battlements between the Lieutenant's Lodgings and the Beauchamp Tower. She takes this exercise whatever the weather and, when it is as windy as it was today, it must be very chilly up there on the roof. Frightening, too, for it overlooks the scaffold site.

There was a moment today when I saw her hooded head above the wall. No one else was around. "Quickly!" I said and, grabbing Frances's hand, I pulled her across the green towards the wall and called in the loudest whisper I could manage, "My lady!"

And the Princess Elizabeth herself actually leaned out and looked straight down at me! Just then a man's voice said, "What is it, my lady?" and she jerked her head back.

I pulled Frances in close to the base of the wall and we pressed ourselves against it. I almost stopped breathing. Voices above murmured for a moment, and then all was quiet.

"What were you thinking of?" demanded Frances.

"I need to talk to her," I said. "I want to give her something."

"What?"

I could have bitten my tongue in two. "Nothing."

"You said something," said Frances. "Something's not nothing." She put on that wheedling face she uses to get her own way. "Tell me!"

I went to walk away, but she grabbed my arm and spun me round. "Tell me!"

But however much she begged, I would not tell her what the something was, and when we met Sal coming back from the water pump, Frances could not resist taunting me. "Guess what Tilly did, Sal?" she said. "You may have three tries."

I told Sal to hold her tongue, but she would not.

"Sat in a puddle?" she said hopefully. "Kissed the Master of the Horse? Set the prisoners free?"

"It is about a prisoner," said Frances and, even though I pinched her hard (and I hope her arm is black and yellow and painful), she proceeded to tell Sal what I had done.

Sal, of course, ran straight home and told Mother, who flew at me and beat me with the soup ladle. Father has gone to apologize to the Gentleman Gaoler, and I am in deep disgrace. I hate Frances, I hate Sal, I hate this house and this book and EVERYTHING.


## 18th April 1554


Now they tell me! At least, William does. Father and he have actually attended the Princess on two occasions. William, of course, only told me to tease me – he will give no more details, except to say that she is courteous and tall. Well, everybody knows that. However, my ears serve me well, and I believe that it is Father's sleeping medicine that she likes to take. I am not surprised she has difficulty sleeping, for the

Queen still suspects that Elizabeth was involved with Wyatt's uprising. Both have been questioned often, Wyatt not as gently as the Princess. However, he said nothing to prove she was at fault, and will certainly say no more, for he was executed a week ago. I feel sorry for his friends and family, as they have no body to bury. Once Wyatt was dead, his body was cut up so the bits could be displayed in different places. I suppose that was done so as many people as possible can see the dreadful result of being a traitor. Today, Tom told me the head has been stolen, probably by Wyatt's followers. Ugh!

Princess Elizabeth will not be released until Queen Mary is sure of her innocence. But I watch and wait for that day to come.

## 21st April 1554

No one, however important, is safe. Not only is the Lady Elizabeth imprisoned here, but also Sir Edward Warner – once a Lieutenant of this very castle! The muttering after church was all about him being involved in Wyatt's rebellion.

# 30th April 1554

More and more beheadings! I truly believed, when Mary came to the throne, that we should have fewer torturings and executions, but it is not so. Once, I enjoyed going to an execution. It was pleasant to all go out together. But now these deaths do sicken me. I talked of this to Father. To my surprise, he understood, and spoke gently. "These days," he said, "the Tower is indeed a bloody place. But understand, Matilda, that the Queen must be secure upon her throne. Until she has a child, the line of succession to the throne is not secure, and she must remove all threats." I asked if the Lady Elizabeth was still a threat. "I think not," he said, "but it is not my opinion that will decide."

I went to see Tom when I knew he would be alone, after the menagerie visitors had gone, but he wasn't there. I bet he was with Sal. Even though we seldom see each other now, the thought of Tom with Sal makes me wild with jealousy. She had asked Mother if she could walk a while outside, as she had a bad head. I'd like to give her a bad head!

Tomorrow I will find Frances. I would like us to be friends again, and I have seen her walk past my house often, so I think she wants it, too. I miss our long talks, and our walks, and I even miss her getting me into trouble. Mother says I am not to lead her astray, but I think it is the other way around. She loves to play tricks on the warders or guards. Once she spread honey on the step old Rufus likes to rest on when no one is watching. He had flies around him all day, and the dogs drove him mad with their sniffing. I laughed and laughed until I realized she had taken the honey from our house.

These days there are often mutterings about our behaviour, but if silver-tongued Frances is around, I am usually safe!

### 3rd May 1554

A murder plot has been discovered! One of Wyatt's men, William Thomas, who was once clerk to King Edward's council, is to be hanged, drawn and quartered at Tyburn because he planned to murder the Queen. Father was called to see him when he tried to kill himself. It's not surprising, for he has already been put to the rack, and must prefer death to more torture. I have never seen the rack. Sal says she has, but she lies. William told me once, when I was small, that they tie your hands at one end and your feet at the other, then turn a handle, and the machinery pulls your bones apart and you scream and scream. No one would have heard Master Thomas's screams. The rack is in a chamber, close by Little Ease, deep down beneath the White Tower, and those walls are about fifteen feet thick. How cold it must be.

## 19th May 1554

Oh, I am so angry! Today was probably my last ever chance to see Princess Elizabeth, and to give her the letter, and where was I? Sitting like a tree stump halfway up the stairs of the Well Tower, keeping guard while Frances held hands (that's what she says she was doing) with a new young worker from the Mint. She is a lunatic. If Master Lea finds out, she will be whipped within an inch of her life and sent back to the country. The boy will lose his job, of course, which is a good one. And me? I should never be anywhere near the Well Tower. It is too near the Royal lodgings.

But they were not caught. So why am I furious? Because while I was sitting in the dark on a cold, damp stair – for show me a tower that is warm even in summer – Princess Elizabeth was taken under guard to a barge and off upriver.

She is to go to a palace called Woodstock, and will be kept there under what is called house arrest, unable to leave.

The first I knew of it was when I heard gunfire a mile or so away. Some of the people believed she must be free, and cheered her. (The guns were a salute, not an attack.) Tom said Master Worsley's own boat passed her, and he saw people cheering and waving all along the riverbank! Father said the same people who cheered the Princess could be the ones to bring her to her death.

"Why?" I asked.

His voice snapped like a whip. "She is next in line for the throne, child! Do you think Queen Mary will be happy that Elizabeth is more popular than she is?"

I think Father likes the Princess, and fears for her. That is why he was irritated with me, for I am sure I spoke politely. I forgive him. Of course, I shall not tell him so!

### 20th May 1554

Frances told me something I did not know. Yesterday, the day Princess Elizabeth left the Tower, was the anniversary of the beheading of her mother. How glad she must have been to leave.

But the little letter ... maybe I should have told Father about it, and asked for his help. But if I do that now, he will be angry that I kept it secret all this time. He is very irritable at the moment, and I think he worries about Mother. The women spend much time with her, and they feel her belly and whisper and tut-tut to each other. I pray all will be well when her time comes.

I am amazed to see how full of words my book is – over three quarters! I will form my letters as small as I can from now on.

## 25th July 1554

Queen Mary will be excited, for last week Prince Philip sailed into Southampton. Sal heard the news from Tom. The prince's arrival must have been a truly magnificent sight, for the Spaniards have sent more than a hundred ships! He has brought with him hundreds and hundreds of nobles and servants. Imagine how much baggage there will be for all those people. The horses! The clothes! The money! Frances and I spent a happy hour imagining what would happen if two young Spanish noblemen should come to the Tower and see two beautiful young ladies (us) and fall in love and take us away to live in palaces. "I would leave everything I own behind," said Frances, "and have all new clothes."

I agreed. "But should I take my book with me?" I mused, "or should I have a scribe to do my writing for me?" Without a doubt, I would keep this pleasure all for myself. How could I let a complete stranger in on my secret thoughts!

For the rest of the day Frances never stopped demanding to know about my book, even though I took her to the menagerie (Mother said I might show Harry the lions one day, and this seemed as good a day as any). Luckily, she did not have the wit to ask Tom, whose tongue would surely have wagged, about my secret. Rather like my parents, I don't think that Frances approves of Tom – and generally won't give him the time of day. I am glad we went to see Tom, for we learned that the Queen's marriage is today in Winchester. Sal does not know about that, and I shall not tell her.

## 30th July 1554

This evening, Sal was sent upstairs to settle Jack, who has a fever. Father says it is mild and he will be well tomorrow. We had several guests (two of whom attended the Queen's marriage) and Mother is so heavy now that she needed much help, so I was able to listen to all the talk about the Royal wedding. This is what happened. The Prince (who it turns out is suddenly a king – his father having given him the kingdoms of Naples and Jerusalem) arrived first at Winchester Cathedral, which is many miles from London – more than 60, I believe. I cannot imagine walking so far – or even riding if I had a horse. When the Queen arrived, they made their confession to the Bishop, and then he performed the marriage service. The Queen has a very old-fashioned ring: plain gold, with no gems. How strange. I should like a gem of every colour. Afterwards, wearing cloth of gold, they each held a sword of honour and walked beneath a canopy held by four knights. Then they sat, which must have been a relief, for there were many prayers and readings. During the mass, which lasted a good hour, they knelt the whole time, which I would find agony, for my knees are bony.

Feasting and dancing has gone on for days since. Wherever Mary and Philip travelled there were fresh celebrations. But not everyone is happy. Father has heard much muttering among Londoners about Spain wanting to rule us. This is from people who wanted Mary to marry an Englishman.

My mother is huge. It must be a giant baby. She is weeks past her time. Surely it will come soon.

## 31st July 1554

When I told Frances about last night, she said, "People who fret over Spaniards wanting to rule us are dolts."

"Why is that?" I asked.

She gave me a most superior look. "Because the Queen herself is half-Spanish, so in a way, Spain already rules us."

She is so simple-minded. You can tell she is from the country.

## 2nd August 1554

It is hard for me to write. Mother is in labour and the women are with her. Father is out and I have escaped up here for a few moments. Mother's cries are loud and terrifying and upset me greatly. And from where I sit in my little room, it doesn't sound like she will survive this ordeal. I pray that she does, and that the little one will be with us soon.

# 29th January 1555

At last Mother is better. I thank God every night for that, and especially so on Sundays. I have not written in my diary for nearly six months. How could I? I go to bed exhausted each night, and simply drop asleep as if I were dead. Our family of six is now eight, for we have beautiful twin girls! Mother was ill for months, but Susy (Susannah, named for the baby who died) and Mary (for the Queen) are fine, fat babies with huge appetites and powerful lungs, and they keep Sal and me busy day and night. Mary, the elder, soon became so strong that it took two of us to put swaddling bands on her, for she fought to be free. I was all for letting her wave and kick, but Father insisted she be swaddled. "Do you want a sister with crooked limbs?" he would bellow.

Oh, I do love them, but I have such little time. I have not seen Tom, apart from in church, for months. Even though Mother is now up and about the house, it is so cold and frosty that I would rather stay in and feed babies before the fire. She has been pleased with me, and calls me "little mother", which made Frances shriek with laughter. I do not often see Frances these days. She does not care for children.

William has become quite soft since Susy and Mary were born, and I almost like him. Father was cheerful today and told me that Sir Edward Warner (the old Lieutenant, who has been imprisoned here since last April) has been released. He had to pay up £300 though. It made me wonder how many people would not have been executed if they had owned such a sum.

The Lady Elizabeth's letter is now tucked into the month of May 1554 – the last time she was here in the Tower. I think she will never sit on the English throne, so it may be she will never come here again. For Queen Mary is to have a child – a prince and heir. William let this slip, and I am not supposed to know it.

## 20th March 1555

Dreadful happenings! Bishops are being burned, and it is on the orders of the Queen. How can she burn holy men? I do not understand. In the last few weeks there have been several burnings in London. I have never been to a burning, and do not wish to, but I have smelled one and found it disgusting. How Mother can stand it I do not know – her nose is so delicate that she could smell when I even looked at Tom (which I have not done for some while). These churchmen were accused of heresy, which means they did not agree with how Mary wishes us to worship. Heretics are always burned. Often, a bag of gunpowder is hung round the victim's neck – it helps them to die quickly when the fire makes it explode. One poor bishop's gunpowder did not explode, and people say he died in terrible, horrifying agony. I thought Mary would be a good queen. But I was wrong – she is not a merciful one.

Now everyone knows she is expecting a baby.


## Later


Poor Bishop Latimer was a prisoner here and a few days ago he was taken to Oxford to be tried for heresy. He will probably burn too, along with all the others. And I wonder if that will make Protestants who have refused to worship as Catholics change their minds. I think, in their shoes, that I would. I would be afraid of the fire.

## 24th April 1555

There was gossip that the Queen is not truly pregnant. But she has put a stop to all that by appearing yesterday at a window in Hampton Court with a very swollen belly. It was St George's Day. I must write smaller. I have few pages left in my diary. Perhaps I should save them for important days.

## 27th August 1555

If such terrible things were not being done in the name of God and the Queen, I would be more sorry for Mary. Many weeks have passed since the Royal baby was due, and now it seems there will not be one. It was a phantom – something that never is and never was! And now Philip is leaving her, to visit the Netherlands. I would leave her, too – many more men and women have been burned at the stake. There cannot be many Protestants left. Even

Princess Elizabeth, who is staying at court for a while, attends mass every day. She has had to hide her Protestant beliefs, and very wise I think she is.

## 18th October 1555

If I had not stopped to argue with Sal, and if I had not called to Tom as I went past the menagerie, and then stopped to watch the lions feed. If I had just done as I was told and gone straight to the poulterer, I might have – no, would have – seen the Lady Elizabeth as she rode to her own home in Hertfordshire. She has the Queen's blessing, and is a free woman. I heard the bells ringing, but took no notice until I saw the crowds. Too late. When I told Father, he said he was glad I missed her. "I hear the people clapped and cheered her and bells were rung," he said. I told him I believed that was true, and he said, "Do the fools not realize what danger they put the Lady Elizabeth in? If the Queen should ever fear that the Lady was becoming too popular, her life would be worth very little, especially as there is no heir to the throne."

"Nor ever likely to be," said William. Father told him to hold his tongue about such matters. I smiled at William, which annoyed him.

# 26th October 1555

William is much kinder to me these days. He said I will one day become a good housewife. And so I will, if I ever marry. That is years away, and none of us are even considering who would be a good husband for me. (When we do, I just hope we all agree!) For now, Mother needs my help more than ever with Susy and Mary, and I secretly suspect that if God is willing we shall soon have another member of the family. Sal suspects, too, I know, and keeps bleating that we need another servant. She is right.

Father was distressed to hear that Bishop Latimer has been burned as a heretic, and another Bishop, Master Ridley of London, was burned with him. Thomas Cranmer, the Protestant Archbishop, was forced to watch. The Queen wanted him to see what will happen to him if he persists in his Protestant ways, and hoped it would change his mind.

William told me Latimer died bravely and, fortunately for him, quickly. He stayed strong to the end, crying out, "Be of good comfort, Master Ridley, and play the man! We shall this day light such a candle, by God's grace, in England, as I trust shall never be put out." (I like those words and have memorized them.) Poor Master Ridley suffered very badly in the flames. My skin prickles when I think of it. I am very careful to do the right thing always in church.

## 26th March 1556

Jack is now six, Harry three and the twins are eighteen months old and wear me out!! I have no time to write these days and go to bed exhausted. The new baby was born much too early, but he is strong and will live, we are sure. He is called Edward, after the baby before me, who died when he was barely two. I wanted to call him Thomas, but Father barked at me, "We are not giving him the same name as that dung-boy." I had not realized that Mother discussed my friends with Father. I should not have thought it that important.

We have just heard that Archbishop Thomas Cranmer has been burned. His behaviour has been very strange. One day he would sign a paper renouncing Protestantism and say he would become a Catholic. Another day he would change his mind. He kept doing that, and I thought him weak and guessed he was doing it to try to save his own life. Indeed, the night before he died, he wrote a recantation, saying he gave up Protestantism (again). However, in the end, perhaps because he knew he was to die anyway, he stayed true to his Protestant faith, and told all those listening that he took back what he had written. As the fire was lit, he held up his right hand. "This was the hand that wrote it," he declared, "and therefore shall it suffer first punishment." Then he thrust it into the flames crying, "This hand hath offended." I think he meant it offended God. Anyway, in no time he was dead. Another death, to add to all the men and women, rich and poor, who have been burned for their faith.

## 28th April 1556

I must write down a horrible thing I heard. The new Archbishop of Canterbury is called Reginald Pole. One of the Yeoman Warders said that Pole's mother, Margaret, was beheaded in 1541 on Tower Green. Well, it's not quite clear exactly where she was beheaded. She refused to kneel and put her head on the block because that was for traitors, and she shouted, "I am no traitor!" She told the executioner that if he wanted her head he would have to get it off the best way he could. And he did! The warder said she ran around, and the executioner chopped and hacked as if he was after a chicken.

# 31st December 1556

It is so cold that I think my ink might freeze. Discovered I am good at sewing, if it is not mending, and I like it. Mother is pleased and lets me make pretty things for the twins, while Sal does the mending. That girl becomes more and more sly as time passes, but I no longer worry or fret about her seeing Tom.

There have been many burnings this year. The Queen is still alone – Philip does not seem to want to return to England. Tower Hill has had more executions than usual, and we have hordes of prisoners. I have heard city dwellers call this place the Bloody Tower, and they do not just refer to that little tower next to the Lieutenant's garden. They mean the whole Tower of London. My home. You would think a woman's reign would be a gentle reign – but it is all death and fear. She has no heir though, which encourages me to hope that maybe. . . No, if I write more it would be treason.

## 7th April 1557

I saw a horrible sight today, by the river at Wapping. A crowd had gathered, so I went down to the shore and pushed my way through to see what was happening. Seven men accused of robbery at sea were tied to a stake while the water was low. The tide came in and it was dreadful to hear their cries as it came ever higher. One brave man deliberately thrust his head underwater to try to drown himself quickly, but he must have panicked. His head came up and he choked and spluttered, then screamed for mercy. I hope never to see the like again and that, by writing it down, the sight will leave my mind.

## 7th June 1557

King Philip has finally come back to England, but the story goes (though I cannot believe a man of noble birth would do such a thing) that he said he would only come back to the

Queen if she agreed to make war on France. She must have been thrilled to see him because every bell in London rang that day for hours. Needless to say, we are at war with France.

## 1st January 1558

Bad news. I am sorry to say so, but the Queen is pregnant. The baby is due in March, but her husband has returned to the Netherlands and has been gone six months so far this time.

Now Elizabeth will never be queen and the burnings will go on and on until Mary runs out of heretics. Unless it is not a baby, but the wind. Is it treason to say that? Probably, but I do not care. I have kept my book safely for nearly five years and apart from Father seeing it once, nobody knows about it (Tom is sure to have forgotten) and I hide it well. I do take out the letter sometimes. It is my secret, and I am not allowed many of them!

# 7th September 1558

I am eighteen years old and today I think back to when I first had this book. Tom was the only person I wanted to be with then. I remember the day I laughed when he said he would become Keeper of the Royal Menagerie! Poor Tom. He still looks after the beasts, and I expect his shovel is as busy as ever. I seldom see him now – we seem to have grown apart. I spend all my spare time, such as it is, with Frances. We go into the city together, to the market, and just walk round looking at people's clothes and seeing everything that goes on. Sometimes William comes with us, which I do not care for much. Frances does not seem to mind at all – in fact I think she rather likes him (strange!). I work hard in the house – Mother is much easier to get on with these days. I told her she had changed. She laughed. "I have not changed," she said. "You have grown up!" The little ones take up most of my time, but I do not mind. I love them dearly, and they love me, too. One day, I will be married and have children of my own. I shall like that. Father never mentions the possibility of marriage. Frances does, often.

The Queen is unwell. (There was no baby – again.)

## 26th October 1558

Much muttering about the Queen's poor health today. It is so exciting to think that we may soon have a new monarch, one who I know will be a good queen. (Though of course, I am sorry for Mary's bad health.)

## 15th November 1558

Sick as she is, and often barely able to open her eyes, the Queen still wishes to burn heretics. It is said that more than 300 have perished horribly in the flames. I wonder, though, if the burnings have been her will alone. I confess I have never given this a thought before. I remember Lady Jane Grey and how men plotted and used her for their own ends. There are probably men who encourage Mary, in the name of God, to do the things she does. I feel hot and uncomfortable now. I have said such bad things about her.

# 18th November 1558

Mary is dead and THE LADY ELIZABETH IS QUEEN! Oh, I am so excited! One thing I know is that before her coronation, the Queen must spend at least one night in the Tower of London. Surely, this time, when she is here without guards and moving about freely, surely this time I may make my curtsey and give her the letter? I will keep it on me always, just in case, tucked into my bodice.

Now the burnings will stop, I am sure. One thing is certain: England will be Protestant once more (how we do bounce back and forth!) and Frances thinks that the Lady – no, Queen Elizabeth will let people worship the Lord as they wish, whether Protestant or Catholic. I like that idea. Which will I be? I scarcely know myself.

## 21st November 1558

We are told that when Mary's ring was taken to Princess Elizabeth at Hatfield and she realized she was now queen, she knelt and said, "This is the Lord's doing. It is marvellous in our eyes." She actually said it in Latin, which I do not know, but William told me what it meant. I think she must have been very relieved indeed. At last she is free of the threat of being imprisoned. Or worse.

## 5th December 1558

She came, and now she's gone. Queen Elizabeth. She stayed in the Tower for several days sorting out her Council, which I did not expect, and I have not even seen her, let alone had a chance to make my curtsey. All I heard were the guns saluting her as she arrived. My bad luck was to have been ill and to endure Father's leeches, and now my face has spots. I screamed when Harry told me, for I thought it was the pox, but Father laughed, saying, "Anyone who can make that much noise is not very ill!"

William has been insufferable and even came to my room, trying to act the physician. I would not let him touch me. He looked around and I was afraid he might poke about and find my book but, "'Tis a mess," was all he said. And so would his room be if Sal did not tidy it for him.

I will still have a chance to see and (I pray) speak with the Queen before her coronation, although I know she will probably be busy with her clothes and jewels.

## 14th January 1559, Coronation Day

I have just watched Queen Elizabeth ride in a litter, with the curtains pulled back so all could see her, out of the gates of the Tower of London. The joyous shouts that went up when the crowds outside first saw her were wonderful to hear. Sal, who was in the Lion Tower with Tom, said even the lions roared their approval as the Queen passed! Everyone is so happy, including me!

My big chance came, and I took it. Last night, some dogs were fighting over something outside (an injured rat and good riddance) and Mother sent me to chase them away before they woke the children or William, who was dozing by the fire. I went unwillingly but once outside, I heard a shout. A royal page ran towards me.

"Are you from the physician's household?" he called. I nodded. "Fetch Master Middleton's apprentice at once," he said, "and bring him to the Queen's apartments." He added that William was to bring Father's small medicine chest.

An imp took charge of my tongue. "My brother is not at home," I said, "but I often assist my father. I know what to bring." I slipped into the house. William snored noisily. I went into Father's room and picked up his medicine chest. I was glad it was the small one. I could not have carried the larger. "What are you doing?" Mother demanded. I told her Father had sent for his chest and the messenger was outside. I went straight to where the page waited.

"Make haste," he said. "The Queen needs to sleep and cannot. Master Middleton gave her a draught that helped her once before, and she has not forgotten." He took me into the Lieutenant's Lodgings, where I have never been. I had no time to look about and we rushed from room to room until we reached a closed door. The page knocked and the door was opened.

I will never forget what I saw – the Queen, in a simple gown, and my father, standing side by side. She looked amused. He looked appalled. Then the Queen said, "Your apprentice, Master Middleton?" He spluttered, "I – I. . ." and went so red that I thought he might explode. This was my chance – the one I had waited years for. Thrusting the chest into Father's arms, I curtsied, then knelt before the Queen. "Your Majesty, I have something for you. I have kept it for several years, and I believe it is your own." Father's mouth fell open as he listened to me tell of my book and how it came to me, and of how I believed it had belonged to Her Majesty's mother, Anne Boleyn. The missing pages, the scratched-out letters. . . The Queen listened in silence.

Finally, I reached into my bodice and took out the tiny fold of paper. It was creased and warm. The Queen held out her hand for it. She looked at the seal which, of course, was unbroken, then turned it over and ran a fingertip across the tearstained word which must once have clearly read "Elizabeth".

"You have kept this safe for me?"

I swallowed. "Yes, Majesty."

The Queen reached out, took my hand and raised me up. "Your name?"

"Tilly – Matilda Middleton, Majesty."

She turned to Father. "Your daughter is a true and faithful subject, Master Middleton." Then she looked at me. "We will speak again, Matilda. For the present, I have much to occupy me. Goodnight."

Father watched me as I backed away. I watched the Queen. She turned the letter over and over, then picked up a small black book – maybe a prayer book – and slipped it inside. Patting the book, she murmured, "I will read it when I am alone."

I raced home, my heart thumping. I was glad Father still had his sleeping draught to prepare – I hoped he would calm down before he saw me again. He did not, but he dared not punish me, for I had pleased the Queen. And now, as I write these words into the final page of my book, I shall not mind if he demands to see it, for I have no secrets now.

I do wish I'd remembered to tell the Queen that we share a birthday. Perhaps when I see her next, for I have a feeling I will. . .

# Historical note

Henry VIII's first wife, Catherine of Aragon, was originally married to Henry's brother, Prince Arthur. When Arthur died, the Pope in Rome gave Henry permission to marry Catherine.

At first, they were happy together, but Henry desperately wanted a son to succeed him as king. Catherine had only one child who lived – the Princess Mary. Hopes of having a son faded as Catherine grew older, and the couple grew apart. Henry fell in love with Anne Boleyn and decided that he must divorce Catherine and marry Anne.

The Pope refused an annulment, which would have put an end to Henry and Catherine's marriage, so Henry took matters into his own hands and divorced Catherine. He married Anne and, in the same year, she had a baby girl, the Princess Elizabeth. In less than two years, Anne was executed for being unfaithful to the King.

Henry's quarrel with the Pope caused a complete break with the Catholic Church in Rome, and resulted in Henry making himself Supreme Head of the Church in England. The Pope's power in England was over.

During the next few years, Henry closed down the monasteries and confiscated their riches and lands. Anyone who opposed him was severely punished.

There were great changes afoot in the country's religious life. People were trying to reform the Catholic Church. The new Protestants (people who were protesting against the old ways) wanted to make services simpler, and easier for ordinary people to understand. This movement was called the Reformation. Henry, although he'd broken with Rome, remained a Catholic in every way, except that he refused to obey the Pope.

His next marriage to Jane Seymour produced what he'd always wanted – a son, Edward. Sadly, Jane Seymour died soon after the birth, and Henry's next three marriages were childless.

In 1547, Henry died, and his son became King Edward VI. He was a studious, intelligent boy, and grew up staunchly Protestant. During his six-year reign, he provided all churches with an English-language Bible, which meant everybody could understand it, and made the Roman Catholic mass illegal. Religious statues were removed and wall paintings were whitewashed over.

Edward's health was poor, and when it became clear that he was soon going to die, his council began to tackle the problem of who was to succeed him. His half-sister, Mary, clearly had a strong claim to the throne, but she was a Catholic. Edward didn't want her undoing all his work on behalf of the Protestant Church.

The power-hungry Duke of Northumberland had great plans. He married his own son, Guilford Dudley, to Lady Jane Grey. She was Henry VIII's great-niece, and was next in line to the throne after Mary and Elizabeth.

Northumberland was in a very strong position. He was Lord President of the Council while Edward was still a child, and exerted great influence over the young king. Soon, Edward had signed a form of will called "My Device for the Succession" which named Lady Jane Grey as his successor. Now Northumberland could foresee a time when his son, Jane's husband, would be king. More power would come to the Northumberland family.

The sickly Edward died at the age of fifteen, and Lady Jane Grey was proclaimed queen. Mary Tudor immediately reclaimed the throne for herself and, with the will of the people behind her, succeeded.

Now Mary set about restoring England to the Catholic Church of Rome, and imprisoned some of the most important Protestants. She married a Catholic Prince of Spain, then began punishing heretics – those who would not follow what she declared was England's true religion. Punishment was usually death by fire, and she soon become known as Bloody Mary. Around 300 men and women, including many priests, were burned at the stake before her death in 1558.

Mary and Philip had no children, and the crown passed to Henry's second daughter, Elizabeth. She had a more tolerant and open attitude towards religion, and was much loved by her people. England prospered under her reign, and became a great power. Elizabeth I was one of England's most successful rulers and, since she remained single all her life, she was the last of the Tudor monarchs.

# Timeline

**1509** Henry VIII marries Catherine of Aragon.

**1516** Henry and Catherine's daughter, Mary, is born.

**1531** Henry VIII declares himself head of the Church in England.

**1533** Henry and Anne Boleyn marry in a secret ceremony.

**September 7** Anne Boleyn gives birth to Elizabeth.

**1534** The Act of Supremacy. Henry VIII is recognized by Parliament as the supreme head of the Church of England.

**1536**

**January 7** Catherine of Aragon dies.

**May 19** Anne Boleyn is executed on Tower Green, in the Tower of London.

**1537** Jane Seymour gives birth to a male heir, Edward, who later becomes King Edward VI.

Lady Jane Grey is born.

**1547** Henry VIII dies at the age of 55.

Henry's son, Edward VI, becomes king. He is nine years old.

**1553**

**May 21** Lady Jane Grey is forced to marry Guilford Dudley, son of the Duke of Northumberland.

**June 21** Edward VI names Lady Jane Grey as his successor.

**July 6** Edward dies at Greenwich Palace.

**July 10** Lady Jane Grey is proclaimed Queen of England.

**July 19** Lady Jane Grey is deposed, after being uncrowned queen for just nine days.

Mary Tudor, daughter of Henry VIII and Catherine of Aragon, becomes Queen Mary I.

**July 25** The Duke of Northumberland and his sons, including Guilford, are imprisoned in the Tower of London.

**August 22** The Duke of Northumberland is executed on Tower Hill.

**October 1** Mary I is crowned queen.

**November 14** Lady Jane Grey and Guilford Dudley are tried and condemned to death.

**1554**

**January 12** Queen Mary signs a marriage treaty with Prince Philip of Spain.

**January** Sir Thomas Wyatt raises an army and begins a rebellion against Queen Mary and the Spanish marriage.

**February 7** Wyatt surrenders.

**February 12** Lady Jane Grey and Guilford Dudley are executed, Jane on Tower Green, and Guilford on Tower Hill.

**February 23** Lady Jane Grey's father, the Duke of Suffolk, is executed on Tower Hill.

**March 18** Princess Elizabeth is imprisoned in the Tower of London.

**April 11** Sir Thomas Wyatt is executed on Tower Hill.

**May 19** Princess Elizabeth leaves the Tower and moves to the palace at Woodstock, where she is kept under house arrest.

**July 25** Queen Mary marries Philip of Spain at Winchester Cathedral.

**1555** The Catholic Queen Mary persecutes Protestants.

**February 9** John Hooper, Bishop of Gloucester, is burned at the stake for heresy.

**October 16** Hugh Latimer, Bishop of Worcester, and Nicholas Ridley, Bishop of London, are both burned at the stake in Oxford.

**October 18** Princess Elizabeth is permitted to return to her home at Hatfield.

**1556** Persecution of Protestants continues.

**February 14** Thomas Cranmer, Archbishop of Canterbury, is removed from office.

**March 21** Cranmer is burned at Oxford.

**April** Reginald Pole replaces Cranmer as the new Archbishop of Canterbury.

**1557** The persecution of Protestants continues.

**June 7** England declares war on France.

**1558** Further persecution of Protestants.

**January 7** The French capture Calais from the English, who have held it for over 200 years.

**November 17** Queen Mary I dies at St James's Palace, aged 42.

Queen Elizabeth I accedes to the throne and reigns until her death in 1603.

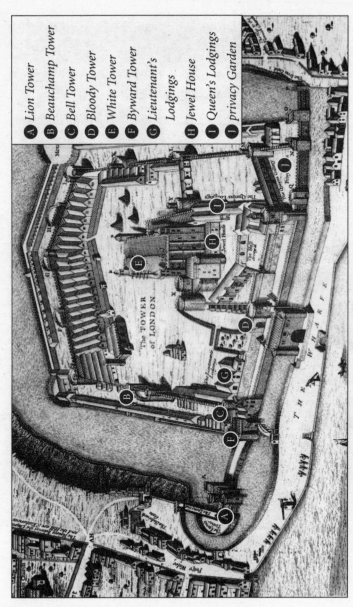

A plan of the Tower of London. The key shows several of the places mentioned in this book.

**A** Lion Tower
**B** Beauchamp Tower
**C** Bell Tower
**D** Bloody Tower
**E** White Tower
**F** Byward Tower
**G** Lieutenant's Lodgings
**H** Jewel House
**I** Queen's Lodgings
**J** privacy Garden

King Philip and Queen Mary.

A portrait of Princess Elizabeth.

The Tower of London from the River Thames.

just rights and priviledges, the honour and conservation of Parliament, in their ancient and just power, the preservation of this poore Church, in her truth, peace, and patrimony, and the settlement of this distracted, and distressed people, under the ancient laws, and in their native liberties, and when thou hast done all this in mercy for them, O Lord, fill their hearts with thankfulnesse, and with religious dutifull obedience to thee and thy Commandements all their dayes: So Amen, Lord Jesus, and I beseech thee receive my soule to mercy. Our Father, &c.

A seventeenth-century woodcut showing traitors being executed on Tower Hill.

A Victorian painting showing the execution of Lady Jane Grey.

The Lady Jane. Proclaimed Queen ~

The Lady Jane and Fecknam a Preist

The Lady Jane Beheaded in y͡e Tower ~

Woodcut illustrations showing Lady Jane Grey's short reign, imprisonment and death.

Scenes from the life of Queen Elizabeth.

A London street during the reign of Elizabeth I.

# Picture acknowledgments

P 137    Plan of the Tower of London, Topham Picturepoint
P 138    Philip of Spain and Mary I, Topham Picturepoint
P 139    Princess Elizabeth, Topham Picturepoint
P 140    Tower of London, Topham Picturepoint
P 141    Executions on Tower Hill, Private Collection/Bridgeman Art Library
P 142    Execution of Lady Jane Grey, Delaroche, National Gallery, London, UK/ Bridgeman Art Library
P 143    Woodcut of scenes from life of Lady Jane Grey, Topham Picturepoint
P 144    Woodcut of scenes from life of Elizabeth I, Topham Picturepoint
P 145    London Street, Cassell's History, Mary Evans Picture Library

Experience history first-hand with My Story –
a series of vividly imagined accounts of life in the past.

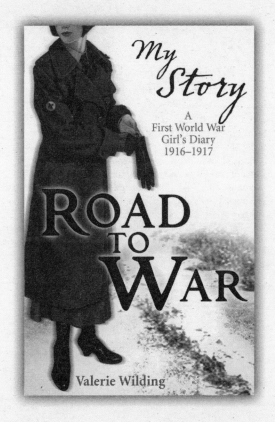

It's 1917 and the **Great War rages** in Europe.
When **Daffy Rowntree's** brother goes missing in
action she refuses to **sit safely** in **England**,
and **determines** to do something **to help** win the war.
Soon she finds herself in the **mud** and **horror** of the
**battlefields** of France, driving an ambulance
transporting the wounded **of the trenches...**

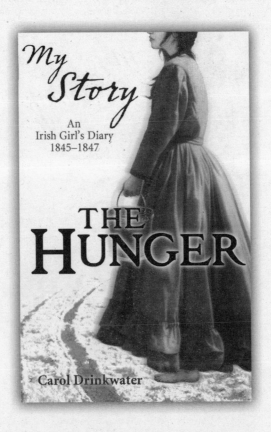

*My Story*

An
Irish Girl's Diary
1845–1847

# THE HUNGER

Carol Drinkwater

It's 1845 and blight has destroyed the precious
potato crop leaving Ireland starving.
Phyllis works hard to support her struggling family,
but when her mother's health deteriorates
she sets off in search of her rebel brother
and is soon swept up in the fight for
a free and fair Ireland...

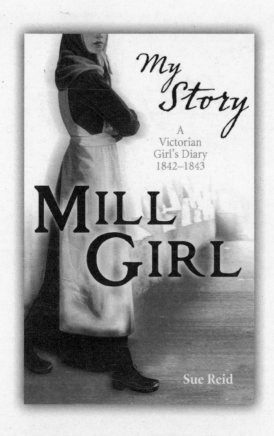

My Story

A Victorian Girl's Diary 1842–1843

MILL GIRL

Sue Reid

In spring 1842 Eliza is shocked when
she is sent to work in the Manchester cotton
mills – the noisy, suffocating mills. The work is
backbreaking and dangerous – and when she sees her
friends' lives wrecked by poverty, sickness
and unrest, Eliza realizes she must fight to escape
the fate of a mill girl...

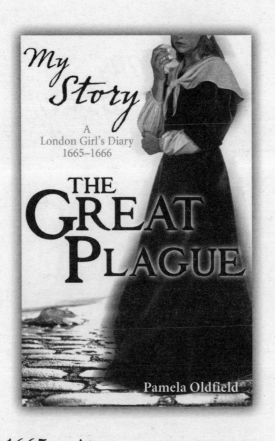

My Story

A
London Girl's Diary
1665–1666

THE
GREAT
PLAGUE

Pamela Oldfield

It's 1665 and **Alice** is looking forward to being
back in **London**. But the **plague**
is **spreading quickly**, and as each day passes
more **red crosses** appear on doors.
When her aunt is **struck down** with **the plague**,
she is forced to make a **decision**
that could **change her life forever...**

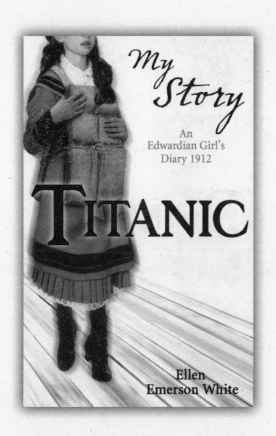

*My Story*

An Edwardian Girl's Diary 1912

# TITANIC

Ellen Emerson White

**Margaret Anne dreams** of leaving the orphanage **behind**, and she can hardly believe her **luck** when she is chosen to accompany **wealthy** Mrs Carstairs aboard the **great** Titanic.

But when the passengers are woken on a **freezing night** in April 1912, she finds herself caught up in an **unimaginable nightmare...**

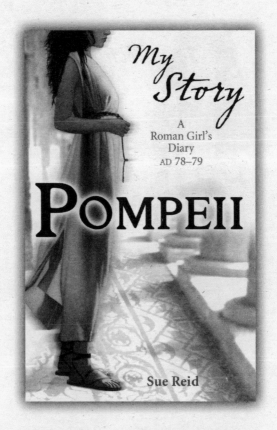

*My Story*

A
Roman Girl's
Diary
AD 78–79

# POMPEII

Sue Reid

It's August AD 78 and **Claudia** is at
the **Forum in Pompeii**. It's a day of
**strange encounters** and even odder portents.
When the **ground shakes** Claudia is
convinced it is a **bad omen**. What does it all mean?
And why is she so disturbed by **Vesuvius**,
the great volcano that looms over the city...

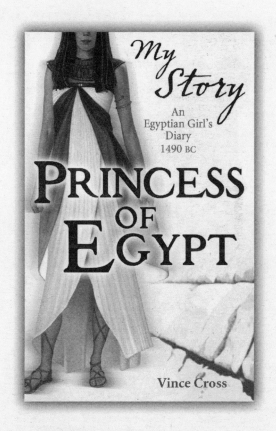

*My Story*

An Egyptian Girl's Diary 1490 BC

# PRINCESS OF EGYPT

Vince Cross

It's 1490 BC and **Asha**, daughter of **King Thutmose**, lives a carefree life at the royal court in **Thebes**. But when a **prophecy** foretells that 'a **young woman** will prove to be the best man in the **Two Kingdoms**', she's caught up in a **world** of **plots** and **danger**...

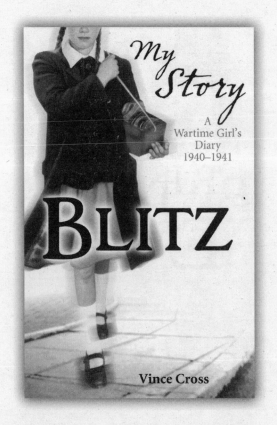

**My Story**

A Wartime Girl's Diary 1940–1941

**BLITZ**

Vince Cross

It's 1940 and with London under fire Edie and her little brother are evacuated to Wales. Miles from home and missing her family, Edie is determined to be strong, but when life in the countryside proves tougher than in the capital she is torn between obeying her parents and protecting her brother...

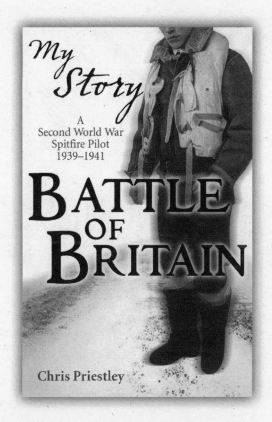

My Story

A
Second World War
Spitfire Pilot
1939–1941

BATTLE
OF
BRITAIN

Chris Priestley

It's 1939 and Harry Woods is a
Spitfire pilot in the RAF. When his friend
Lenny loses his leg in a dogfight with the
Luftwaffe, Harry is determined to fight on.
That is, until his plane is hit and he finds
himself tumbling through the air
high above the English Channel...

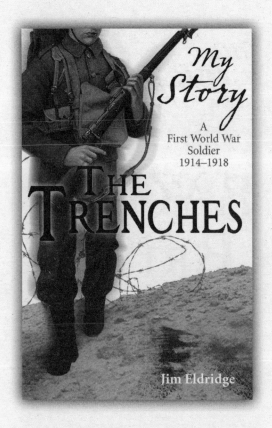

It's 1917 and Billy Stevens is a telegraph
operator stationed near Ypres. The Great War
has been raging for three years when Billy finds
himself taking part in the deadly Big Push forward.
But he is shocked to discover that the bullets
of his fellow soldiers aren't just
aimed at the enemy...

Coming soon – the sequel to *Bloody Tower*

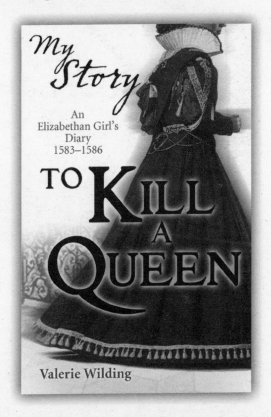

It's the 1580s. Queen Elizabeth's enemies
plot to kill her and place Mary Queen of Scots
on the throne. While Kitty's father works on secret
projects for Elizabeth, her brother's mixing with
suspicious characters. As Mary's supporters
edge closer by the minute, Kitty fears the worst ... that
they'll all be thrown into the Tower.